A Jacana book

Timbuktu, Timbuktu

A Selection of Works from the

Caine Prize for African Writing 2001

First published in 2002 by **Jacana**
5 St Peter Rd
Bellevue
2198
www.jacana.co.za
e-mail: marketing@jacana.co.za

This edition © **Jacana**

ISBN 1-919931-06-6

Cover design by **Disturbance**
2nd floor Innesdale
101 Innes Rd
Morningside
Durban
e-mail: disturb@mweb.co.za

Page design by **Lynda Harvey**

Printed by **Formeset Printers**
22 Kinghall Ave
Eppindust
Cape Town
7945

Acknowledgements

The publishers would like to thank the following people for their assistance in publishing this book:

The authors, publishers, and translators for their kind permission in allowing their stories to be published in this collection;

Stephen Gray for his generous help and assistance;

Nuruddin Farah's story, *America, Her Bra!* originally appeared in the *New Yorker* of 15 October 2001, under the title *Land Beyond*.

Contents

✳

Speech made by Dan Jacobson at the awards banquet for the Caine Prize 2001 held at the Bodleian Library, Oxford

Judging the entries for this year's Caine Prize for African Writing was an intense and at times a tense experience for all involved. It was difficult for the judges to draw up the 'long short list'; more difficult still, obviously, to draw up the official short list, which was published several weeks ago; and there were times this afternoon when I wondered if we would ever be able to agree on a solitary winner in time for this occasion. However we eventually did succeed in coming to a unanimous decision, and I will not keep you waiting for long before I announce the name of the winning author.

But now I do want to make a couple of observations to you – the first which is in fact a kind of paradox. The stories we judged had just one thing in common: each of them differed so greatly from all the others. This is true even of the short list, let alone of the many entries that were regretfully put aside at an earlier stage of the proceedings. Our short list contained stories written by men and women from northern, southern and central Africa, and from its eastern and its western coasts; and in tone, style, intention and subject matter the contending tales varied as greatly from one another as they did in their regional provenance.

Their variety was not the consequence of any attempt on our part to present a representative selection of what was on offer; nor did it spring from a wish to show the breadth of our taste by including as many kinds of story – naturalistic or fantastic, comic or grim – as we could. Nothing of the kind. To the best of our abilities we tried to judge each item on its merits. What we found ourselves producing nevertheless, was a microcosm of the size and variousness of the continent itself, and hence of its many peoples and climates, and of the presence within it of bewilderingly disparate cultural influences and states of development.

My second observation is of a different kind, though it is closely connected to what I have just said. Several people to whom I mentioned my interest in the prize – Africans as well as Europeans among them – were plainly sceptical about the value, the worthwhileness, of what my fellow-judges and I were trying to do. These sceptics were not philistines, they were not (in their own minds anyway) dismissive of the importance of the arts in the life of any community. But in the face of the terrible problems that currently ravage many parts of the continent – disease, war, corruption, tyranny, famine – they spoke almost as if it were improper for us to be giving attention to works of the imagination. By that phrase I mean writing which did not directly seek to alleviate or even to describe the continent's ills, but sprang instead from a handful of individuals whose prime wish was to understand and to articulate their inner life – in its fantastic and speculative as well as its commonplace aspects – and in so doing to make their inner life meaningful to others.

A modest ambition? In some ways, yes. In other ways, far from it. To illustrate what I mean allow me to read you a short extract from a story by one of the writers whose work we have discussed this afternoon. The hero of the story, Lomba, is a young Nigerian journalist and would-be novelist; he is about to cover for his newspaper a demonstration which he (rightly) suspects is going to be brutally repressed by the military authorities. (He is in fact flung into jail before the day is over.) Before setting out he is instructed in the realities of his situation by his editor, James who asks him if he has finished his novel, which of course Lomba admits he has not done. So James speaks again.

'But let us assume you've finished it. Let us assume it's a good book, potentially great. Let us say you've found a publisher for it – we're talking theory now, because in reality you won't find a publisher for it. Not in this country… You won't find a publisher because it'll be economically unwise for any publisher to waste his scarce newsprint to publish a novel which nobody will buy because people are too poor, too illiterate, and too busy trying to keep out of the way of the police and the army to read… But forget all that. Say you find an indulgent publisher to publish your book, and because you are sure your book is good you'd want to enter it for a competition – and the most obvious

8

competition for someone from a Commonwealth country is of course the Commonwealth Literary Prize. But you can't do it.'

'And why not?' Lomba asks. He stands up and moves to the window, away from James, so that they stare at each other, the table between them, like antagonists.

'Because Nigeria was thrown out of the Commonwealth of Nations early this morning. It was on the BBC... You can't write with chains on your hands.' James' voice is soft now, apologetic. 'Sorry I had to be brutal. But you needed it. We are all in this together.'

Ladies and gentlemen, I have much pleasure in announcing that the Caine Prize for African Writing for 2001 has been awarded by the judges to Helon Habila of Nigeria, author of the story, 'Love Poems'.

Dan Jacobson

Helon Habila

Love Poems

In the middle of his second year in prison Lomba got access to
pencil and paper and he started a diary. It was not easy. He had to
write in secret, mostly in the early mornings when the night warders,
tired of peeping through the door bars, waited impatiently for the
morning shift. Most of the entries he simply headed with the days of
the week; the exact dates, when he used them, were often incorrect.
The first entry was in July 1997, a Friday.

Friday, July 1997
Today I begin a diary, to say all the things I want to say, to myself,
because here in prison there is no one to listen. I express myself. It
stops me from standing in the centre of this narrow cell and screaming
at the top of my voice. It stops me from jumping up suddenly and
bashing my head repeatedly against the wall. Prison chains not so
much your hands and feet as it does your voice.

I express myself. I let my mind soar above these walls to bring back
distant, exotic bricks with which I seek to build a more endurable cell
within this cell. Prison. Misprison. Dis. Un. Prisoner. See? I write of
my state in words of derision, aiming thereby to reduce the weight of
these walls from my shoulders, to rediscover my nullified individuality. Here in prison loss of self is often expressed as anger. Anger is the
baffled prisoner's attempt to re-crystallise his slowly dissolving self.
The anger creeps on you, like twilight edging out the day. It builds in
you silently until one day it explodes in violence, surprising you. I saw
it happen in my first month in prison. A prisoner, without provocation,
had attacked an unwary warder at the toilets. The prisoner had come
out of a bath-stall and there was the warder before him, monitoring the
morning ablutions. Suddenly the prisoner leaped upon him, pulling
him by the neck to the ground, grinding him into the black, slimy
water that ran in the gutter from the toilets. He pummeled the surprised face repeatedly until other warders came and dragged him away.
They beat him to a pulp before throwing him into solitary.

Sometimes the anger leaves you as suddenly as it appeared; then you enter a state of tranquil acceptance. You realize the absolute puerility of your anger: it was nothing but acid, cancer, eating away your bowels in the dark. You accept the inescapability of your fate; and with that, you learn the craft of cunning. You learn ways of surviving – surviving the mindless banality of the walls around you, the incessant harassment from the warders; you learn to hide money in your anus, to hold a cigarette inside your mouth without wetting it. And each day survived is a victory against the jailor, a blow struck for freedom.

My anger lasted a whole year. I remember the exact day it left me. It was a Saturday, a day after a failed escape attempt by two convicted murderers. The warders were more than usually brutal that day; the inmates were on tenterhooks, not knowing from where the next blow would come. We were lined up in rows in our cell, waiting for hours to be addressed by the prison superintendent. When he came his scowl was hard as rock, his eyes were red and singeing, like fire. He paced up and down before us, systematically flagellating us with his harsh, staccato sentences. We listened, our heads bowed, our hearts quaking.

When he left, an inmate, just back from a week in solitary, broke down and began to weep. His hands shook, as if with a life of their own. "What's going to happen next?" he wailed, going from person to person, looking into each face, not waiting for an answer. "We'll be punished. If I go back there I'll die. I can't. I can't." Now he was standing before me, a skinny mass of eczema inflammations, and ringworm, and snot. He couldn't be more than twenty. I thought, what did he do to end up in this dungeon? Then, without thinking, I reached out and patted his shoulder. I even smiled. With a confidence I did not feel I said kindly, "No one will take you back."

He collapsed into my arms, soaking my shirt with snot and tears and saliva. "Everything will be all right," I repeated over and over. That was the day the anger left me.

In the over two months that he wrote before he was discovered and his diary seized, Lomba managed to put in quite a large number of entries. Most of them were poems, and letters to various persons from his by now hazy, pre-prison life – letters he can't have meant to send. There were also long soliloquies and desultory interior monologues. The poems were mostly love poems; fugitive lines from poets he had read in school: Donne, Shakespeare, Graves, Eliot, etc. Some were his original compositions rewritten from memory, but a lot were fresh creations – tortured sentimental effusions to women he had known and admired, and perhaps loved. Of course they might be imaginary beings, fabricated in the smithy of his prison-fevered mind. One of the poems reads like a prayer to a much doubted, but fervently hoped for God:

Lord, I've had days black as pitch
And nights crimson as blood

But they have passed over me, like water
Let this one also pass over me, lightly,
Like a smooth rock rolling down the hill,
Down my back, my skin, like soothing water.

That, he wrote, was the prayer on his lips the day the cell door opened without warning and the superintendent, flanked by two baton carrying warders, entered.

Monday, September.
I had waited for this; perversely anticipated it with each day that passed, with each surreptitious sentence that I wrote. I knew it was me he came for when he stood there, looking bigger than life, bigger than the low, narrow cell. The two dogs with him licked their chops and growled menacingly. Their eyes roved hungrily over the petrified inmates caught sitting, or standing, or crouching; laughing, frowning, scratching – like figures in a movie still.

"Lomba, step forward!" his voice rang out suddenly. In the frozen silence it sounded like glass breaking on concrete, but harsher, without the tinkling. I was on my mattress on the floor, my back propped against the damp wall. I stood up. I stepped forward.

He turned the scowl on me. "So, Lomba. You are."

"Yes. I am Lomba," I said. My voice did not fail me. Then he nodded, almost imperceptibly, to the two dogs. They bounded forward eagerly, like game hounds scenting a rabbit; one went to a tiny crevice low in the wall, almost hidden by my mattress. He threw aside the mattress and poked two fingers into the triangular crack. He came out with a thick roll of papers. He looked triumphant as he handed it to the superintendent. Their informer had been exact. The other hound reached unerringly into a tiny hole in the sagging, rain-designed ceiling and brought out another tube of papers.

"Search. More!" the superintendent barked. He unrolled the papers. He appeared surprised at the number of sheets in his hands.

13

I was. I didn't know I had written so much. When they were through with the holes and crevices the dogs turned their noses to my personal effects. They picked my mattress and shook and sniffed and poked. They ripped off the tattered cloth on its back. There were no papers there. They took the pillow-cum-rucksack (a jeans trouser-leg cut off at mid-thigh and knotted at the ankle) and poured out the contents onto the floor. Two threadbare shirts, one trouser, one plastic comb, one toothbrush, one half-used soap, and a pencil. This is the sum of my life, I thought, this is what I've finally shrunk to, the detritus after the explosion: a comb, a toothbrush, two shirts, one trouser, and a pencil. They swooped on the pencil before it had finished rolling on the floor, almost knocking heads in their haste.

"A pencil!" the superintendent said, shaking his head, exaggerating his amazement. The prisoners were standing in a tight, silent arc. He walked the length of the arc, displaying the papers and pencil, clucking his tongue. "Papers. And pencil. In prison. Can you believe that? In my prison!"

I was sandwiched between the two hounds, watching the drama in silence. I felt removed from it all. Now the superintendent finally turned to me. He bent a little at the waist, pushing his face into mine. I smelt his grating smell; I picked out the white roots beneath his carefully dyed moustache. "I will ask. Once. Who gave you. Papers?" He spoke like that, in jerky, truncated sentences. I shook my head. I did my best to meet his red-hot glare. "I don't know."

Some of the inmates gasped, shocked; they mistook my answer for reckless intrepidity. They thought I was foolishly trying to protect my source. But in a few other eyes I saw sympathy. They understood that I had really forgotten from where the papers came.

"Hmm," the superintendent growled. His eyes were on the papers in his hands, he kept folding and unfolding them. I was surprised he had not pounced on me yet. Maybe he was giving me a spell to reconsider my hopeless decision to protect whoever it was I was protecting. The papers. They might have blown in through the door bars on the sentinel wind that sometimes patrolled the prison yard in the evenings. Maybe a sympathetic warder, seeing my yearning for self-expression emblazoned like neon on my face, had secretly thrust the roll of papers into my hands as he passed me in the yard. Maybe – and this seems more probable – I bought them from another inmate (anything can be bought here in prison: from marijuana to a gun). But I had forgotten.

In prison, memory short-circuit is an ally to be cultivated at all costs.

"I repeat. My question. Who gave you the papers?" he thundered into my face, spraying me with spit. I shook my head. "I have forgotten."

I did not see it, but he must have nodded to one of the hounds. All I felt was the crushing blow on the back of my neck, where it meets the head. I pitched forward, stunned by pain and the unexpectedness of it. My face struck the door bars and I fell before the superintendent's boots. I saw blood where my face had touched the floor. I waited. I stared, mesmerized, at the reflection of my eyes in the high gloss of the boots' toecaps. One boot rose and descended on my neck, grinding my face into the floor.

"So, you won't. Talk. You think you are. Tough," he shouted. "You are. Wrong. Twenty years! That is how long I have been dealing with miserable bastards like you. Let this be an example to all of you. Don't. Think you can deceive me. We have our sources of information. You can't. This insect will be taken to solitary and he will be properly dealt with. Until. He is willing to. Talk."

I imagined his eyes rolling balefully round the tight, narrow cell, branding each of the sixty inmates separately. The boot pressed down harder on my neck; I felt a tooth bend at the root.

"Don't think because you are political. Detainees you are untouchable. Wrong. You are all rats. Saboteurs. Anti-government rats. That is all. Rats."

But the superintendent was too well versed in the ways of torture to throw me into solitary that very day. I waited two days before they came and blindfolded me and took me away to the solitary section. In the night. Forty-eight hours. In the first twenty-four hours I waited with my eyes fixed to the door, bracing myself whenever it opened; but it was only the cooks bringing the meal, or the number-check warders come to count the inmates for the night, or the slop-disposal team. In the second twenty-four hours I bowed my head into my chest and refused to look up. I was tired. I refused to eat or speak or move.

I was rehearsing for solitary.

They came, around ten in the night. The two hounds. Banging their batons on the door bars, shouting my name, cursing and kicking at anyone in their path. I hastened to my feet before they reached me, my trouser-leg rucksack clutched like a shield in my hands. The light of their torch on my face was like a blow.

"Lomba!"

"Come here! Move!"

"Oya, out. Now!"

I moved, stepping high over the stirring bodies on the floor. A light fell on my rucksack.

"What's that in your hand, eh? Where you think say you dey carry am go? Bring am. Come here! Move!"

Outside. The cell door clanked shut behind us. All the compounds were in darkness. Only security lights from poles shone at the sentry posts. In the distance the prison wall loomed huge and merciless, like a mountain. Broken bottles. Barbed wire. Then they threw the blindfold over my head. My hands instinctively started to rise, but they were held and forced behind me and cuffed.

"Follow me."

One was before me, the other was behind, prodding me with his baton. I followed the footsteps, stumbling. At first it was easy to say where we were. There were eight compounds within the prison yard; ours was the only one reserved for political detainees. There were four other Awaiting Trial Men's compounds surrounding ours. Of the three compounds for convicted criminals, one was for lifers and one, situated far away from the other compounds, was for condemned criminals. Now we had passed the central lawn where the warders conducted their morning parade. We turned left towards the convicted prisoners' compounds, then right towards... we turned right again, then straight...I followed the boots, now totally disoriented. I realised that the forced march had no purpose to it, or rather its purpose was not to reach anywhere immediately. It was part of the torture.

I walked. On and on. I bumped into the front warder whenever he stopped abruptly.

"What? You no de see? Idiot!"

Sometimes I heard their voices exchanging pleasantries and amused chuckles with other warders. We marched for over thirty minutes; my slippered feet were chipped and bloody from hitting into stones. My arms locked behind me robbed me of balance and often I fell down, then I'd be prodded and kicked. At some places – near the light poles – I was able to see brief shimmers of light. At other places the darkness was thick as walls, and eerie. I recalled the shuffling, chain-clanging steps we heard late at nights through our cell window. Reluctant, sad steps. Hanging victims going to the hanging room, or their ghosts returning.

We'd lie in the dark, stricken by immobility, as the shuffling grew distant and finally faded away. Now we were on concrete, like a corridor.

The steps in front halted. I waited. I heard metal knock against metal, then the creaking of hinges. A hand took my wrist, cold metal touched me as the handcuffs was unlocked. My hands felt light with relief. I must have been standing right before the cell door because when a hand on my back pushed me forward I stumbled inside. I was still blindfolded, but I felt the consistency of the darkness change: it grew thicker, I had to wade through it to feel the walls, the bunk, the walls and walls. That was all: walls so close together that I felt like a man in a hole. I reached down and touched the bunk. I sat down. I heard the door close. I heard footsteps retreating. When I removed the blindfold the darkness remained the same, only now a little air touched my face. I closed my eyes. I don't know how long I remained like that, hunched forward on the bunk, my sore, throbbing feet on the floor, my elbows on my knees, my eyes closed. As if realising how close I was to tears, the smells got up from their corners, shook the dust off their buttocks and lined up to make my acquaintance – to distract me from my sad thoughts.

I shook their hands one by one: Loneliness Smell, Anger Smell, Waiting Smell, Masturbation Smell, Fear Smell. The most noticeable was Fear Smell, it filled the tiny room from floor to ceiling, edging out the others. I did not cry. I opened my lips and slowly, like a Buddhist chanting his mantra, I prayed:

Let this one also pass over me, lightly,
Like a smooth rock rolling down the hill
Down my back, my skin, like soothing water.

He was in solitary for three days. This is how he described the cell in his diary: *The floor was about six feet by ten, and the ceiling was about seven feet from the floor. There were exactly two pieces of furniture: the iron bunk with its tattered, lice-ridden mat, and the slop bucket in the corner.* His only contacts with the outside were in the nights when his mess of beans, once daily, at six p.m., was pushed into the cell through a tiny flap at the bottom of the wrought iron door, and at precisely eight p.m. when the cell door opened for him to take out the slop bucket and replace it with a fresh one. He wrote that the only way he distinguished night from day was by the movement of his bowels – in hunger or in purgation.

Then on the third day, late in the evening, things began to happen. Like Nichodemus, the superintendent came to him, covertly, seeking knowledge.

Third Day. Solitary Cell.

When I heard metal touch the lock on the door I sat down from my blind pacing. I composed my countenance. The door opened, bringing in unaccustomed rays of light. I blinked. *"Oh, sweet light. May your face meeting mine bring me good fortune."* When my eyes adjusted to the light, the superintendent was standing on the threshold – the cell entrance was a tight, lighted frame around his looming form. He advanced into the cell and stood in the centre, before my disadvantaged position on the bunk. His legs were planted apart, like an A. He looked like a cartoon figure: his jodhpurs-like uniform trousers emphasised the skinniness of his calves, where they disappeared into the glass glossy boots.

His stomach bulged and hung like a belted sack. He cleared his voice. When I looked at his face I saw his blubber lips twitching with the effort of attempted smile. But he couldn't quite carry it off. He started to speak, then stopped abruptly and began to pace the tiny space before the bunk. When he returned to his original position he stopped. Now I noticed the sheaf of papers in his hands. He gestured in my face with it.

"These. Are the. Your papers." His English was more disfigured than usual: soaking wet with the effort of saying whatever it was he wanted to say. "I read. All. I read your file again. Also. You are journalist. This is your second year. Here. Awaiting trial. For organising violence. Demonstration against. Anti-government demonstration against the military legal government." He did not thunder as usual.

"It is not true."

"Eh?" the surprise on his face was comical. "You deny?"

"I did not organise the demonstration. I went there a reporter."

"Well..." He shrugged. "That is not my business. The truth. Will come out at your. Trial."

"But when will that be? I have been forgotten. I am not allowed a lawyer, or visitors. I have been awaiting trial for two years now..."

"Do you complain? Look. Twenty years I've worked in prisons all over this country. Nigeria. North. South. East. West. Twenty years. Don't be stupid. Sometimes it is better this way. How. Can you win a case against government? Wait. Hope."

Now he lowered his voice, like a conspirator, "Maybe there'll be another coup, eh? Maybe the leader will collapse and die; he is mortal after all. Maybe a civilian government will come. Then. There will be amnesty for all political prisoners. Amnesty. Don't worry. Enjoy yourself."

I looked at him planted before me like a tree, his hands clasped behind him, the pâpier-maché smile on his lips. *Enjoy yourself.* I turned the phrase over and over in my mind.

When I lay to sleep rats kept me awake, and mosquitoes, and lice, and hunger, and loneliness. The rats bit at my toes and scuttled around in the low ceiling, sometimes falling onto my face from the holes in the ceiling. *Enjoy yourself.*

"Your papers," he said, thrusting them at me once more. I was not sure if he was offering them to me. "I read them. All. Poems. Letters. Poems, no problem. The letters, illegal. I burned them. Prisoners sometimes smuggle out letters to the press to make us look foolish. Embarrass the government. But the poems are harmless. Love poems. And diaries. You wrote the poems for your girl, isn't it?" He bent forward; clapped a hand on my shoulder. I realised with wonder that the man, in his awkward, flatfooted way, was making overtures of friendship to me. My eyes fell on the boot that had stepped on my neck just five days ago. What did he want?

"Perhaps because I work in Prison. I wear uniform. You think I don't know poetry, eh? Soyinka, Okigbo, Shakespeare."

It was apparent that he wanted to talk about poems, but he was finding it hard to begin.

"What do you want?" I asked.

He drew back to his full height. "I write poems too. Sometimes," he added quickly when the wonder grew and grew on my face. He dipped his hand into his jacket pocket and came out with a foolscap paper. He unfolded it and handed it to me. "Read."

It was a poem; handwritten. The title was written in capital letters: "MY LOVE FOR YOU". Like a man in a dream I ran my eyes over the bold squiggles. After the first stanza I saw that it was a thinly veiled imitation of one of my poems. I sensed his waiting. He was hardly breathing. I let him wait. Lord, I can't remember another time when I had felt so good. So powerful. I was Samuel Johnson and he was an aspiring poet waiting anxiously for my verdict, asking tremulously: "Sir, is it poetry, is it Pindar?"

I wanted to say, with as much sarcasm as I could put into my voice: "Sir, your poem is both original and interesting, but the part that is interesting is not original, and the part that is original is not interesting." But all I said was, "Not bad, you need to work on it some more."

The eagerness went out of his face and for a fleeting moment the scowl returned. "I promised my lady a poem. She is educated, you know. A teacher. You will write a poem for me. For my lady."

"You want me to write a poem for you?" I tried to mask the surprise, the confusion and, yes, the eagerness in my voice. He was offering me a chance to write.

"I am glad you understand. Her name is Janice. She has been to the university. She has class. Not like other girls. She teaches in my son's school. That is how we met."

Even jailors fall in love, I thought inanely.

"At first she didn't take me seriously. She thought I only wanted to use her and dump her. And. Also. We are of different religion. She is Christian, I am Muslim. But no problem. I love her. But she still doubted. I did not know what to do. Then I saw one of your poems... yes, this one." He handed me the poem. "It said everything I wanted to tell her."

It was one of my early poems, rewritten from memory.

" 'Three Words'. I gave it to her yesterday when I took her out."

"You gave her my poem."

"Yes."

"You...you told her you wrote it?"

"Yes, yes, of course. I wrote it again in my own hand," he said, unabashed. He had been speaking in a rush; now he drew himself together and, as though to reassert his authority, began to pace the room, speaking in a subdued, measured tone.

"I can make life easy for you here. I am the prison superintendent. There is nothing I cannot do, if I want. So write. The poem. For me."

There is nothing I cannot do: You can get me cigarettes, I am sure, and food. You can remove me from solitary. But can you stand me outside these walls free under the stars? Can you connect the tips of my upraised arms to the stars so that the surge of liberty passes down my body to the soft downy grass beneath my feet?

I asked for paper and pencil. And a book to read.

He was removed from the solitary section that day. The pencil and papers came, the book too. But not the one he had asked for. He wanted Wole Soyinka's prison notes, *The Man Died*; but when it came it was *A Brief History of West Africa*. While writing the poems in the cell Lomba would sometimes let his mind wander; he'd picture the superintendent and his lady out on a date, how he'd bring out the poem and unfold it and hand it to her and say boldly, "I wrote it for you. Myself."

They sit outside on the verandah at her suggestion. The light from the hanging, wind-swayed Chinese lanterns falls softly on them. The breeze blowing from the lagoon below smells fresh to her nostrils; she loves its dampness on her bare arms and face. She looks across the circular table, with its vase holding a single rose petal, at him. He appears nervous. A thin film of sweat covers his forehead. He removes his cap and dabs at his forehead with a white handkerchief.

"Do you like it, a Chinese restaurant?" he asks, like a father anxious to please his favourite child. It is their first outing together. He pestered her until she gave in. Sometimes she is at a loss what to make of his attentions. She sighs. She turns her plump face to the deep blue lagoon. A white boat with dark stripes on its sides speeds past; a figure is crouched inside, almost invisible. Her light, flower patterned gown shivers in the light breeze. She watches him covertly. He handles his chopsticks awkwardly, but determinedly.

"Waiter!" he barks, his mouth full of fish, startling her. "Bring another bottle of wine!"

"No. I am all right, really," she says firmly, putting down her chopsticks.

After the meal, which has been quite delicious, he lifts the tiny, wine filled porcelain cup before him and says: "To you. And me."

She sips her drink, avoiding his eyes.

"I love you, Janice. Very much. I know you think I am not serious. That I only want to suck. The juice and throw away the peel. No." He suddenly dips his hand into the pocket of his well-ironed white kaftan and brings out a yellow paper.

"Read and see." He pushes the paper across the table to her. "I wrote it. For you. A poem."

She opens the paper. It smells faintly of sandalwood. She looks at the title: "Three Words". She reaches past the vase with its single, white rose petal, past the wine bottle, the wine glasses, and covers his hairy hand with hers briefly. "Thank you."

She reads the poem, shifting in her seat towards the swaying light of the lantern:

Three Words

When I hear the waterfall clarity of your laughter,
When I see the twilight softness of your eyes,

I feel like draping you all over myself, like a cloak,
To be warmed by your warmth.

Your flower petal innocence, your perennial

Sapling resilience – your endless charms

All these set my mind on wild flights of fancy:
I add word unto word,
I compare adjectives and coin exotic phrases
But they all seem jaded, corny, unworthy
Of saying all I want to say to you.

So I take refuge in these simple words
Trusting my tone, my hand in yours, when I
Whisper them, to add depth and new
Twists of meaning to them. Three words:
I love you.

With his third or fourth poem for the superintendent, Lomba
began to send Janice cryptic messages. She seemed to possess an insa-
tiable appetite for love poems. Everyday a warder came to the cell, in
the evenings, with the same request from the superintendent: "The
poem." When he finally ran out of original poems, Lomba began to
plagiarise the masters from memory. Here are the opening lines of one:

Janice, your beauty is to me
Like those treasures of gold...

Another one starts:

I wonder, my heart, what you and I
Did till we loved...

But it was Lomba's bowdlerisation of Sappho's "Ode" that brought
the superintendent to the cell door:

A peer of goddesses she seems to me
The lady who sits over against me
Face to face,
Listening to the sweet tones of my voice,
And the loveliness of my laughing.
It is this that sets my heart fluttering
In my chest,
For if I gaze on you but for a little while

I am no longer master of my voice,
And my tongue lies useless
And a delicate flame runs over my skin
No more do I see with my eyes;
The sweat pours down me
I am all seized with trembling
And I grow paler than the grass
My strength fails me
And I seem little short of dying.

He came to the cell door less than twenty minutes after the poem had reached him, waving the paper in the air, a real smile splitting his granite face.

"Lomba, come out!" he hollered through the iron bars. Lomba was lying on his wafer-thin mattress, on his back, trying to imagine figures out of the rain designs on the ceiling. The door officer hastily threw open the door.

The superintendent threw a friendly arm over Lomba's shoulders. He was unable to stand still. He walked Lomba up and down the grassy courtyard.

"This poem. Excellent. With this poem. After. I'll ask her for marriage." He was incoherent in his excitement. He raised the paper and read aloud the first line, straining his eyes in the dying light: " 'A peer of goddesses she seems to me'. Yes. Excellent. She will be happy. Do you think I should ask her for. Marriage. Today?"

He stood before Lomba, bent forward expectantly, his legs planted in their characteristic A-formation.

"Why not?" Lomba answered. A passing warder stared at the superintendent and the prisoner curiously. The twilight fell dully on the broken bottles studded in the concrete of the prison wall.

"Yes. Why not. Good." The superintendent walked up and down, his hands clasped behind him, his head bowed in thought. Finally he stopped before Lomba and declared gravely: "Tonight. I'll ask her."

Lomba smiled at him, sadly. The superintendent saw the smile; he did not see the sadness.

"Good. You are happy. I am happy too. I'll send you a packet of cigarette. Two packets. Today. Enjoy. Now go back inside."

He turned abruptly on his heels and marched away.

September
Janice came to see me two days after I wrote her the Sappho. I

23

thought, she has discovered my secret messages, my scriptive Morse tucked innocently in the lines of the poems I've written her.

Two o'clock is compulsory siesta time. The opening of the cell door brought me awake. My limbs felt heavy and lifeless. I feared I might have an infection. The warder came directly to me. "Oya, get up. The superintendent wan see you." His skin was coarse, coal black. He was fat and his speech came out in laboured gasps.

"Oya, get up. Get up," he repeated impatiently.

I was in that lethargic, somnambulistic state condemned people surely fall into when, in total inanition and despair, they await their fate – without fear or hope, because nothing could be changed. No dew-wet finger of light would come poking into the parched gloom of the abyss they tenanted. I did not want to write any more poems for the super-intendent's lover. I did not want any more of his cigarettes. I was tired of being pointed at behind my back, of being whispered about by the other inmates as the superintendent's informer, his fetch-water. I wanted to recover my lost dignity. Now I realise that I really had no "self" to express; that self had flown away from me the day the chains touched my hands; what is left here is nothing but a mass of protrud-ing bones and unkempt hair and tearful eyes; and asshole for shitting and farting; and a penis that in the mornings grows turgid in vain. This leftover self, this sea-bleached wreck panting on the iron-filing sands of the shores of this penal island is nothing but hot air, and hair, and ears cocked, hopeful...

So I said to the warder: "I don't want to see him today. Tell him I'm sick."

The fat face contorted. He raised his baton in Pavlovan response. "What!" But our eyes met. He was smart enough to decipher the bold "No Trespassing" sign written in mine. Smart enough to obey. He moved back, shrugging. "Na you go suffer!" he blustered, and left.

I was aware of the curious eyes staring at me. I closed mine. I willed my mind over the prison walls to other places. Free. I dreamt of stand-ing under the stars, my hands raised, their tips touching the blinking, pulsating electricity of the stars. My naked body surging with the surge. The rain would be falling. There'd be nothing else: just me and rain and stars and my feet on the wet downy grass earthing the elec-tricity of freedom.

He returned almost immediately. There was a smirk on his fat face as he handed me a note. I recognised the superintendent's clumsy scrawl. It was brief, a one-liner: *Janice is here. Come. Now.* Truncated, even in writing. I got up and pulled on my sweat-grimed shirt. I slipped my feet into my old, worn-out slippers. I followed the warder. We passed the parade ground, and the convicted men's compound. An iron gate, far to our right, locked permanently, led to the women's wing of the prison. We passed the old laundry, which now served as a bar- bershop on Saturdays – the prison's sanitation day. A gun-carrying warder opened a tiny door in the huge gate that led into a foreyard where the prison officials had their offices. I had been here before, once, on my first day in prison. There were cars parked before the offices, cadets in their well-starched uniforms came and went, their young faces looking comically stern. Female secretaries with time on their hands stood in the corridors gossiping. The superintendent's office was not far from the gate; a flight of three concrete steps led up to a thick wooden door, which bore the single word: SUPERINTEN- DENT.

My guide knocked on it timidly before turning the handle.

"The superintendent wan see am," he informed the secretary. She barely looked up from her typewriter; she nodded. Her eyes were bored, uncurious.

"Enter," the warder said to me, pointing to a curtained doorway beside the secretary's table. I entered. A lady sat in one of the two vi- sitors' armchairs. Her back to the door; her elbows rested on the huge Formica topped table before her. Janice. She was alone. When she turned I noted that my mental image of her was almost accurate. She was plump. Her face was warm and homely. She came half way out of her chair, turning it slightly so that it faced the other chair. There was a tentative smile on her face as she asked: "Mr Lomba?"

I almost said no, surprised by the "mister". I nodded. She pointed at the empty chair. "Please sit down."

She extended a soft, pudgy hand to me. I took it and marveled at its softness. She was a teacher; the hardness would be in the fingers: the tips of the thumb and the middle finger, and the side of the index fin- ger.

"Muftau... the superintendent will be here soon. He just stepped out," she said. Her voice was clear, a little high-pitched. Her English was correct, each word carefully pronounced and projected. Like in a classroom. I was struck by how clean she looked, squeaky-clean; her skin glowed like a child's after a bath. She had obviously taken a lot of trouble with her appearance: her blue evening dress looked almost new, a slash of red lipstick extended to the left cheek after missing the curve of the lip. She crossed and uncrossed her legs, tapping the left foot on the floor. She was nervous. That was when I realized I had not said a word since I entered.

"Welcome to the prison," I said, unable to think of anything else.

She nodded. "Thank you. I told Muftau I wanted to see you. The poems, I just knew it wasn't him writing them. I went along with it for a while, but later I told him."

She opened the tiny handbag in her lap and took out some papers. The poems. She put them on the table and unfolded them, smoothing out the creases, uncurling the edges. "After the Sappho I decided I must see you. It was my favourite poem in school, and I like your version of it."

"Thank you," I said. I liked her directness, her sense of humour.

"So I told him – look, I know who the writer is, he is one of the prisoners, isn't he? That surprised him. He couldn't figure out how I knew. But I was glad he didn't deny it. I told him that. And if we are getting married, there shouldn't be secrets between us, should there?"

Ah, I thought, so my Sappho has worked the magic. Aloud, I said, "Congratulations."

She nodded. "Thanks. Muftau is a nice person, really, when you get to know. His son, Farouk, was in my class – he's finished now – really, you should see them together. So touching. I know he has his awkward side, and that he was once married – but I don't care. After all, I have a little past too. Who doesn't?" she added the last quickly, as if scared she was revealing too much to a stranger. Her left hand went up and down as she spoke, like a hypnotist, like a conductor. After a brief pause, she continued:

"After all the pain he's been through with his other wife, he deserves some happiness. She was in the hospital a whole year before she died."

Muftau. The superintendent had a name, and a history, maybe even a soul. I looked at his portrait hanging on the wall, he looked young in it, serious faced and smart, like the cadet warders outside. I turned to her and said suddenly and sincerely: "I am glad you came. Thanks."

Her face broke into a wide, dimpled smile. She was actually pretty. A little past her prime, past her sell-by date, but still nice, still viable. "Oh no. I am the one that should be glad. I love meeting poets. I love your poems. Really I do."

"Not all of them are mine."

"I know – but you give them a different feel, a different tone. And also, I discovered your S.O.S. I had to come…" She picked the poems off the table and handed them to me. There were thirteen of them. Seven were my originals, six were purloined. She had carefully underlined in red ink certain lines in some of them – the same line, actually, recurring.

There was a waiting-to-be-congratulated smile on her face as she awaited by comment.

"You noticed," I said.

"Of course I did. S.O.S. It wasn't apparent at first. I began to notice the repetition with the fifth poem. 'Save my soul, a prisoner'."

Save my soul, a prisoner… The first time I put down the words, in the third poem, it had been non-deliberate, I was just making alliteration. Then I began to repeat it in the subsequent poems. But how could I tell her that the message wasn't really for her, or for anyone else? It was for myself, perhaps, written by me to my own soul, to every other soul, the collective soul of the universe.

I said to her; The first time I wrote it an inmate had died. His name was Thomas. No, he wasn't sick. He just started vomiting after the afternoon meal, and before the warders came to take him to the clinic, he died. Just like that. He died. Watching his stiffening face, with the mouth open and the eyes staring, as the inmates took him out of the cell, an irrational fear had gripped me. I saw myself being taken out like that, my lifeless arms dangling, brushing the ground. The fear made me sit down, shaking uncontrollably amidst the flurry of movements and voices excited by the tragedy. I was scared. I felt certain I was going to end up like that. Have you ever felt like that, certain that you were going to die? No? I did. I was going to die. My body would end up in some anonymous mortuary, and later in an unmarked grave, and no one would know. No one would care. It happens everyday here. I am a political detainee, if I die I am just one antagonist less. That was when I wrote the S.O.S. It was just a message in a bottle, thrown without much hope into the sea…I stopped speaking when my hands started to shake. I wanted to put them in my pocket to hide them from her. But she had seen it. She left her seat and came to me. She took both my hands in hers.

"You'll not die. You'll get out alive. One day it will all be over," she said. Her perfume, mixed with her female smell, rose into my nostrils; flowery, musky. I had forgotten the last time a woman had stood so close to me. Sometimes, in our cell, when the wind blows from the female prison, we'll catch distant sounds of female screams and shouts and even laughter. That is the closest we ever come to women. Only when the wind blows, at the right time, in the right direction. Her hands on mine, her smell, her presence, acted like fire on some huge, prehistoric glacier locked deep in my chest. And when her hand touched my head and the back of my neck, I wept.

27

When the superintendent returned my sobbing face was buried in Janice's ample bosom, her hands were on my head, patting, consoling, like a mother, all the while cooing softly, "One day it will finish."

I pulled away from her. She gave me her handkerchief.

"What is going on? Why is he crying?"

He was standing just within the door – his voice was curious, with a hint of jealousy. I wiped my eyes; I subdued my body's spasms. He advanced slowly into the room and went round to his seat. He remained standing, his hairy hands resting on the table.

"Why is he crying?" he repeated to Janice.

"Because he is a prisoner," Janice replied simply. She was still standing beside me, facing the superintentent.

"Well. So. Is he realising that just now?"

"Don't be so unkind, Muftau."

I returned the handkerchief to her.

"Muftau, you must help him."

"Help. How?"

"You are the prison superintendent. There's a lot you can do."

"But I can't help him. He is a political detainee. He has not even been tried."

"And you know that he is never going to be tried. He will be kept here forever, forgotten." Her voice became sharp and indignant. The superintendent drew back his seat and sat down. His eyes were lowered. When he looked up, he said earnestly, "Janice. There's nothing anyone can do for him. I'll be implicating myself. Besides, his lot is far easier than that of other inmates. I give him things. Cigarettes. Soap. Books. And I let him. Write."

"How can you be so unfeeling? Put yourself in his shoes – two years away from friends, from family, without the power to do anything you wish to do. Two years in CHAINS! How can you talk of cigarettes and soap, as if that were substitute enough for all that he has lost?" She was like a teacher confronting an erring student. Her left hand tapped the table for emphasis as she spoke.

"Well." He looked cowed. His scowl alternated rapidly with a smile. He stared at his portrait on the wall behind her. He spoke in a rush, "Well. I could have done something. Two weeks ago. The Amnesty International. People came. You know, white men. They wanted names of. Political detainees held. Without trial. To pressure the government to release them."

"Well?"

"Well." He still avoided her stare. His eyes touched mine and hastily passed. He picked a pen and twirled it between his fingers; the pen slipped out of his fingers and fell to the floor.

"I didn't. Couldn't. You know… I thought he was comfortable. And, he was writing the poems, for you…" His voice was almost pleading. Surprisingly, I felt no anger at him. He was just Man. Man in his basic, rudimentary state, easily moved by the powerful emotions, like love, lust, anger, greed, fear; but totally dumb to the finer, acquired emotions like pity and mercy and humour, and justice.

Janice slowly picked up her bag from the table. There was enormous dignity to her movements. She clasped the bag under her left arm. Her words were slow, almost sad, "I see now that I've made a mistake. You are not really the man I thought you were…"

"Janice." He stood up and started coming round to her, but a gesture stopped him.

"No. Let me finish. I want you to contact these people. Give them his name. If you can't do that, then forget you ever knew me."

Her hand brushed my arm as she passed me to the door. He started after her, then stopped half way across the room. We stared in silence at the curtained doorway, listening to the sound of her heels on the bare floor till it finally died away. He returned slowly to his seat and slumped into it. The wood creaked audibly in the quiet office.

"Go," he said, not looking at me.

The above is the last entry in Lomba's diary. There's no record of how far the superintendent went to help him regain his freedom, but like he told Janice there was very little he could have done for a political detainee – especially since about a week after that meeting a coup was attempted against the military leader, General Sani Abacha, by some officers close to him. There was an immediate crackdown on all pro-democracy activists, and the prisons all over the country swelled with political detainees. A lot of those already in detention were transferred randomly to other prisons around the country – for security reasons. Lomba was among them. He was transferred to Agodi Prison in Ibadan. From there he was moved to the far north, to a small desert town called Gashuwa. There was no record of him after that.

A lot of these political prisoners died in detention, although only the prominent ones made the headlines – people like Moshood Abiola and General Yar Adua.

But somehow it is hard to imagine that Lomba died, a lot seem to point to the contrary. His diaries, his economical expressions, show a very sedulous character at work. A survivor. The years in prison must have taught him not to hope too much, not to despair too much, that for the prisoner nothing kills as surely as too much hope or too much despair. He had learned to survive in tiny atoms, piece-meal, a day at a time. It is probable that in 1998, when the military dictator, Abacha, died, and his successor, General Abdulsalam Abubakar, dared to open the gates to democracy, and to liberty for the political detainees, Lomba was in the ranks of those released.

This is how it might have happened: Lomba was seated in a dingy cell in Gashuwa, his eyes closed, his mind soaring above the glass studded prison walls, mingling with the stars and the rain in elemental union of freedom; then the door clanked open, and when he opened his eyes it was Liberty standing over him, smiling kindly, extending an arm.

And Liberty said softly, "Come. It is time to go."

And they left, arm in arm.

✳

The Iron Gate

The men begin to arrive early in the morning. It is drizzling, a remainder from last night's downpour. The sky is still overcast, waiting with more rain. They arrive singly and in groups, picking their way carefully through the wet elephant grass and pools of brown water that cover the dirt road leading to the company gate. They walk silently, save for an occasional cough, as if scared of disturbing the quiet that covers the sleepy neighbourhood like a blanket. Occasionally an early car roars past, splashing water at them; they'll swear and shake their fists at its receding posterior. Sometimes the clouds shift to expose the sun's progress in the sky. And soon the men can see the company's high walls with barbed wire and broken bottles on top, and the huge iron gate at the front. In the illusory morning light the gate looms huge and menacing, like a live thing, and for a moment the men's hearts sink; but when they remember the distance they've come and the possibilities that may be waiting, they renew their resolve. It is a multi-national oil company, owned by Europeans and Americans and a few Nigerian military officers, and for the past two days its gate has been shut to the over five hundred men that turned up in response to the company's advertisement for ten truck drivers. The company officials were overwhelmed by the excess of response. The men congregate before the big gate, ignoring the drizzle, exchanging handshakes and nods and hopeful words. They look tired even this early in the morning: some are rheumy-eyed from aborted sleep, some are still heady from last night's wine, some are dizzy from accumulated hunger. Almost all are identically dressed in cheap plastic raincoats, some have umbrellas folded beneath their arms. They all carry plastic bags in which their credentials are carefully folded: driver's licences, birth certificates, testimonials and letters of recommendation from driving instructors and past employers. Most of the credentials are mouldy from long storage. The sun is almost free of the clouds now; the rain has ceased. The men keep on coming, already there are over four hundred of them ranged on either sides of the road that passes beneath the gate. They look tiny, like ants, before the big gate. Huge chains and bolts keep it locked from inside, it can only be opened by the uniformed security men whose shed stands just within the gate. It is past ten o'clock now. As the sun grows stronger in the sky, the men become restive; a rumour is making the rounds that today they'll definitely be attended to. They move about, glancing anxiously at one another and at the gate. Some knock on it, they joke loudly, but the jokes are spurious, the laughter strained. They are all too aware that they compete for the same posts. Whenever the gate opens to let a car in or out the men will catch a glimpse of the company's interior: the gleaming cars parked beside the neat lawns; the gushing water-fountains; the buildings white with pink aluminium roofs, looking like giant cakes in the sun. At such moments the men's longing to get in, to be a part of this paradise, will become unbearable and, like a mighty wave breaking on the shore, they will throw themselves at the yawning, beckoning space, moaning with a million unnamed longings, only to be forced back again by the gate closing. Then they will stare at this huge iron barrier; their eyes will desperately measure its towering, barbed-wired height, as if in readiness to scale it. After a while the wild glow will leave their eyes to be replaced by a look of utter dejection, their shoulders will slump under the weight of their despair and their legs will drag beneath them as they mill about with tired determination. And the melee will form again as another car passes. They are like puppets in the hands of a mad and ruthless puppeteer.

Mid-day finds most of them squatting in the grass by the roadsides, some lean against the tall walls on either sides of the gate; a few die-hards still run forward whenever the gate opens, but half-heartedly. They look at one another and in their eyes is the beginning of the realisation that today they might not be attended to after all: soon the working hours will be over; soon they will start the long trek back home. But... the day is not over yet. The rain begins to pour heavily. Those with umbrellas hastily open them and they all stand together in groups, huddled close together like sheep keeping warm. Some of them bring out their lunch packs and start to eat, sharing with those that have none. They eat in silence, furtively, their eyes steadfastly fixed to the gate. They don't want to be caught unawares when the big gate finally opens.

Mia Couto

The Russian Princess

Translated from the Portuguese by Luis Rafael

I'm so sorry, Father, I'm not kneeling properly. You know, Father, it's my leg: it doesn't really go with the rest of my body, this very thin leg that I use on my left.

I've come to confess sins from long ago. My soul's like blood trampled upon. I'm even scared to remember them. Please, Father, listen to me at a slow speed. Be patient. It's a long story. Like I always say: the path the ant makes never ends close by.

Maybe you don't know it, Father, but at one time this town had another life altogether. There was a time when many people from far-away places arrived here. The world's full of places, most of them foreign ones. There're so many of them. The whole of Heaven's filled with their flags. I can't imagine how the angels get around without knocking into all those flags. What d'you say? I must walk inside the story? Yes, I'll walk in. But don't forget: I did ask for a lot of your time, a small lot of your time. You see, Father, life takes a long time.

I must continue, then. At that time a Russian lady also arrived in the town of Manica. Her name was Nadia. They said she was princess in the land where she came from. She came with her husband Yuri, who was also Russian. The two of them came for the gold, like all the other foreigners who came to dig out the riches from under our soil. But like our elders always say: don't run after the chicken with salt in your hand. You see, Father, those mines were the size of a speck of dust. You blew once and there was nothing.

But those Russians did bring with them the bits and pieces of their previous way of life – the luxuries of old times. You should have seen their house, Father. It was full of things. And houseboys? There were more than many. I was already 'assimilated' and I became the head of the houseboys. D'you know what they called me? General Foreman. That was my rank; I was a somebody. I didn't work: I made the others work. I was the only one who attended to the Master and Milady. They spoke to me in a good way, always with respect. Whenever they requested something from me I shouted at the houseboys and ordered them to do it. Yes, I shouted. That was the only way they obeyed. No one started getting that tired feeling just because they felt like it. Or don't you think that when God threw Adam out of Paradise he didn't give him a few kicks?

Those houseboys hated me, Father. I could feel their anger when I took their holidays away from them. I didn't mind. In a way I even liked not being liked. Their anger made me feel fat inside. I felt almost – almost like the boss. I was told that it's a sin to enjoy bossing people around. But I think it's this leg that gives me wicked advice. I've got two legs: one belongs to a saint, the other to the devil. How can I walk in one direction?

Sometimes I overheard the houseboys talking in the back rooms. They were angry about lots of things. They spoke through clenched teeth. As soon as I walked in they'd shut up. They didn't trust me. But I was flattered with the way they distrusted me: I was the master of that fear which made me feel so small. They took revenge. They made fun of me. They were always copying my limp-limp. The bastards laughed. I'm sorry I used a swearword in this place where you're supposed to show respect. But I feel this old anger like it's still happening. I was born with this defect. It was a punishment God had in store for me even before I was made into a person. I know God's all-powerful. But still, Father, d'you think he was fair to me? Am I offending the Holiest One? Well, I am confessing my sins. If I cause too much offence now then Father can add more on the forgiveness side later on.

All right, I'll continue. The days never changed in that house. Sad and quiet. The Master left early for the gold mine – the gold plot, we called it. He only came back at night. The nightest of the night. The Russians never had visitors. The others, the English, the Portuguese, those never stopped by. The princess lived inside her own sadness. She dressed up for visitors even when she was alone at home. I think she visited herself. She always spoke in whispers. If you wanted to hear what she was saying you had to put your ear really close. I would move closer to her, her thin body – I've never seen skin as white as hers. That whiteness took to frequenting my dreams. Even today, the fragrance of that colour makes me shudder.

She had a habit of lingering behind in the small hall and staring up at the clock. She would listen to the dials and the time going drip–drip–drip. It was a clock she'd got from her family. I was the only one allowed to clean it. If that clock were to break, Fortin, it would be as if my whole life had broken. That's what she was always saying to me. I was advised to be careful.

On one of those nights I was lighting the coals in my room at the back. That's when I saw a shadow behind me and got a fright. I looked again and saw it was Milady. She'd brought a candle with her and she walked very slowly towards me. She looked at my room while the light was dancing on all four corners. I didn't know what to do. I was even embarrassed. She'd always seen me in the white uniform that I used for work. And here I was in shorts. With no shirt on, with no respect at all. The princess walked around and then, much to my surprise, sat on my mat. Have you ever? A Russian princess sitting on a mat? She stayed there for a long time, just sitting, and continuing to sit. Then she asked me a question in her funny way of speaking Portuguese: '*So you leeve ghere ah–fter all?*'

I had no answer for her. I even thought she was sick. Her head was getting places all mixed up. 'Milady, it's better for you to go back to the house. This room's not so good for Milady.'

She didn't respond to that. She asked another question: '*Is it goot enough for you?*'

'It's enough for me. All we need is a roof to protect us from the sky.'

She undermined everything I was so sure of. She said only *animas* hid themselves in holes. Each person is its own place – the place from we start sowing our lives. I asked if there were blacks in her country and she laughed and laughed. Oh, Fortin, you ask such odd questions! I was surprised: if there were no blacks then who did all the heavy work? Whites, she said. Whites? She was lying, I thought. After all, how many laws are there in the universe? Could it be that misfortune wasn't distributed according to race? No, I'm not asking you, Father. I'm thinking aloud.

That's how we spoke that night. When she was by the door she asked me if I would show her the hostels where the others lived. At first I said I wouldn't. But deep down I wanted her to go there. So she'd see something more wretched than my own life. And so I obliged. We set out in the dark towards the place reserved only for domestic servants. Princess Nadia was filled with sadness when she saw how they lived. She was so shaken that she began to swop languages. She went skipping from Portuguese back to Russian. Now she understood why the Master wouldn't let her go out. Why he'd never given her permission. It's only so I wouldn't see this misery, she said. I noticed that she was crying. Poor lady. I felt sorry for her. A white woman, so far away from her own people, there in the middle of the bushveld. Yes, for the princess it must've been bush, all of it. The surroundings of the bush. Even the big house always tidied according to her own customs, even her house was a bush-house.

When we returned I pricked myself on one of the micaia thorns. The thorn got deep into my foot. The princess tried to help me but I didn't want her to: 'You can't touch this leg of mine, Milady…'

She understood. She tried to console me; said it wasn't a defect at all. I shouldn't be ashamed of my body. At first I didn't like it. I thought she felt pity for me. Compassion. Nothing more. But after a while I was so lost in her sweetness that I forget the pain on my foot. It seemed like that leg that moved all over the place wasn't mine anymore.

It was from that night onwards the princess started to go out. She started to visit the areas around. She took advantage of the Master's absence and she asked me to show her all the footpaths. One day, Fortin, we'll leave early and go to the mine. Her wishes frightened me. I knew Master's orders. The lady wasn't allowed out.

Until one day the whole thing exploded: 'The other servants have told me that you have been taking walks with the Madam.'

Bastards. They'd complained about me. So I'd know that I was no different from them: I was reduced to size by the same voice. Jealousy is the worst type of snake: it bites with the victim's own teeth.

And so, at that moment, I took a step back: 'It's not because I want to, Master. It's Milady that tells me to.'

See what I did Father? All it took was a second and there I was accusing Milady, betraying her confidence.

'It's the last time it happens. Do you hear that, Fortin?'

We never took to the roads again. The princess asked me, she insisted with me. Only for a short distance, Fortin. But the spirit had left me. And she went back to being a prisoner in the house. She looked like a statue. Even when the Master came home at night she continued to look at the clock in silence. She seemed to see a time that only those who were absent could see. The Master didn't even bother with her: he'd walk straight to the table and ask for a drink. He drank, he ate, he drank, he ate. He didn't notice Milady. It was like he was *sub–existing*. He didn't hit her. Beating up the wife wasn't a thing a prince did. They'd never hit or kill someone, they'd give orders for somebody else to do it. It's we who are destined to work for others that are the hands of their dirty wishes. I always beat up people when I was told to do so. I was a whirlwind of beatings up. I only hit people of my race. Now I look around me and there's no one I can call brother. Not one person. Those blacks don't forget. They're full of grudges, this race of mine. You're also black, Father. You know what I mean. If God's black, Father, then I'll sizzle: I'll never be forgiven. Never ever. What d'you say? Mustn't I talk about God? Why's that, Father? D'you think he can hear me here, so far away from Heaven, and me so small? Can he hear? Wait, Father, I must straighten the way I'm sitting. Blasted leg. It never wants to obey me.

All right, I'm ready to confess more things. It was like I said. Or more correctly: like I was saying. The house of the Russians was story-less. Nothing happened. Only Milady's silence and her whispers. And the clock, which was like a drum sound in the hollow.

Until one day the Master shouted at me about something urgent: 'Call the servants, Fortin. Quick. I want them all outside.'

I got them all together, the houseboys and the kitchen totos and even the fat cook, Nelson Machine.

'We're going to the mine. Quick. Get on the wagon.'

We got to the mine, were given spades and began to dig. Once more the roof of the mine had collapsed. There were men under the ground we were walking on. Some of them were dead already, others were saying goodbye to dear life. The spades went up and down. Nervous spades. We began to see arms coming from inside the sand – they looked like roots made of flesh. There were shouts, there was a whole mix up of different commands and there was dust. The fat cook next to me was pulling an arm, trying to get all the strength to tug out the entire body. But I tell you what: it was a loose arm, it had already been torn away from its body. The cook fell. He was still holding that chunk of arm in his hands. Sitting there just like that he burst out laughing. He looked at me and his laughter was filled with tears. Fatty looked just like a lost child sobbing away.

I couldn't cope, Father. I unabled myself to cope. I know I sinned: I turned my back on all that misfortune. There was too much suffering. One of the houseboys tried to hold me. He insulted me. I turned my face. I didn't want him to see that I was crying.

That year the mine fell a second time. Again, this second time, I walked away from the job of saving lives. I'm no good, Father, I know it. But you've never seen a Hell like that one. We pray to God to save us from Hell when we die. But what difference does it make? We already live in Hell, we walk on its flames and our souls have got all its scars. That's what it was like over there. It was like a farm of blood and sand. We were scared even to walk. Because death was burying itself inside our own eyes. And she was pulling our soul down with her many arms. Why is it my fault? Be honest with me, why is it my fault that I was incapable of shaking little bits of people in a sieve?

I'm not a rescue man. Things happen to me, I don't make things happen. I was thinking about these things on my way home. My eyes didn't even look to the front. It as though I was walking inside my own tears. Then, all of a sudden, I remembered the princess. I seemed to hear her voice asking for help. It was as if she was there, beside each tree, begging on her knees – like I'm doing now. But once again I wouldn't let myself help anyone. Goodness wasn't for me and I walked away.

Back in my room I found it difficult to listen to the world all around me – so full of the beautiful sounds of nightfall. My thoughts were locked in a dark room. That's when her hands came. Slowly they unloosened the obstinate snakes that my arms had become. She spoke to me as if I were a child, the child she'd never had: *'Zhere was éksident in mine, yes?'*

I answered with my head. She pronounced terrible curses in her own language and then left. I went with her. I knew that she suffered more than I did. The princess sat in the lounge and waited with her. She sat in silence. When her master returned she got up slowly. She was holding the glass clock in her hands. The one she had entrusted me to take special care with. She lifted the clock well above her head and with all her strength threw it on the ground. Pieces of glass were scattered everywhere – the floor was covered with glittering grains. She then moved on to break the chinaware. She did this slowly and without shouting. But I knew those bits of glass were cutting her soul open. The Master, yes, he shouted. First in Portuguese. He commanded her to stop. He shouted in their own language. She didn't even hear. And d'you know what she did? No, Father, you can't imagine it. It's even difficult for me to have to tell it. The princess took her shoes off, she stared at her husband and began to dance on top of the broken pieces of glass. She danced, danced, danced. The amount of blood she left behind, Father! I know about it, I was the one who cleaned it up. I took a cloth and cleaned the floor like I was caressing Milady's own body, like I was consoling all her many sorrows. The Master told me to get out and to leave everything as it was. But I refused to. I've got to clean up this blood, Master, I said. I was speaking back to him in a voice which didn't even seem to be mine. Was I showing disobedience? Where did I get that strength that held me close to the ground and made me a prisoner of my own will?

And that's what happened, even though it doesn't sound like the truth. Then all of a sudden a lot of time went by. I don't know if it was because of the glass, but on the next day the lady got sick. She was laid to bed in a separate room. She slept alone. She rested on the sofa while

I made the bed. We spoke. The topic was always the same: she remembered things from her country – the lull–lullabies of when she was a child.

'This sickness Milady, I'm sure it's from missing something too much.'

'My life is zhere. Man I love ghe is in Russia, Fortin.'

My mind danced way – I was pretending. I didn't want to understand.

'Ghis name is Anton. Sat is only mwaster of my gheart.'

I'm imitating the way she spoke. It's not that I want to make fun of her. But that's how I keep her confession, the one about that man she loved. Other secrets came along – she was always offering me the memories of that love she kept so hidden. I was scared in case anyone overheard our conversations. I got the job done quickly so I could get out of that room. But one day she gave me a sealed envelope. It was something I had to be very secret about. No one was allowed to suspect. Ever. She told me to post the letter at the post office in town.

From that day onwards she started giving me letters. One followed the other, and the other, and another. She wrote while she was lying down. The writing on the envelope was shaky because of her high temperature.

But Father: d'you want to know the truth? I never posted those letters. None at all. Not even one. I have sinned and I suffer for it. It was fear that stopped me from obeying like I should have – fear of being caught red–handed with that burning evidence.

The poor lady treated me with all the goodness in her. She believed I was making a sacrifice for her. She'd give me the letters and I'd begin to shake: it was like my fingers were holding the fire. Yes, what I said was correct: the fire. Because that's where all those letters ended. I threw them all in the kitchen coal–stove. All Milady's secrets were burnt over there. I'd hear the fire and it sounded like her own sighs. Bloody hell, Father, I'm getting a cold sweat just from talking about these things that make me feel so ashamed of myself.

And that's how life went on. The lady had less and less strength. I'd walk in the room and she'd look at me. It was as if those blue eyes pierced through me. She never asked if a reply had come. Nothing. Only those eyes questioned me in silent despair, those eyes that had been snatched away from the sky.

The doctor was coming every day. He'd leave the room and shake his eyes. He didn't think there was any hope. The whole house was dark. The curtains were always closed. There were only shadows and

silence. One day I noticed that the door was open by a half slit. It was
Milady peering to see. She waved at me; and I went in. I asked her if
she was getting better. She didn't reply. She sat in front of the mirror
and put scented rice powder on her deathly face – she was cheating
death of its colour. She painted her lips, but she took a long time to get
the paint on the respective lips. Her hands were shaking so much that
she made a red scratch on her nose and on all around the chin. If I'd
been a woman I would have helped but I was a man. I just looked. And
kept to myself.

'Is Milady going out?'

'Vee go to si–tation. You end me.'

'To the station?'

'Yes. Anton comes on ttrain.'

She opened her bag and showed me a letter. She told me it was his
reply. It had taken long but eventually she'd received it. She was shaking the envelope, like children do when they're scared their fantasies
will be taken away. She said something in Russian. Then she spoke in
Portuguese: Anton was coming on the Beira train. He was going to take
her away from there to a very far place.

The lady was raving, I'm sure. It was all make–believe. How could
she have got a reply? Wasn't I the one who used to collect the post? And
hadn't the lady not left the house for much more than many days? And
what's more: weren't the letters addressed to the fire?

We went out to the street, she was holding on to me. I was her walking–stick until we got close to the station. It was here, Father, that I
committed my worst sin. I'm very hard on myself. I don't give myself
a chance. Yes, I'll defend myself against anything except myself. I can
already count on God being my side. Don't you think I'm right,
Father? Then, listen.

The princess's skin was tight against my own body – I was sweating
her own sweat. The lady was on my lap, the whole of her – her whole
abandoned self. Who was that Anton if not I? Yes, I was the one who
made himself into the writer of that letter. Was I deceitful? At the time
I was in favour of it. After all, there wasn't much left of Milady's life.
What did it matter if I helped her fantasies a little? Maybe – who knows
– that bit of madness would help to heal the wound that was stealing
her body away from her. But, Father, have you considered what I was
really trying to be? Was I, Duarte Fortin, general foreman of the houseboys, running away with a white woman, and a princess at that? As if
she would have wanted to go with me, a man with my colour and with
unequal sized legs. There's no doubt about it. I have the soul of an

earthworm. I'm really going to crawl in the other world. My sins ask
for more than many prayers. Pray for me, Father, don't stop praying for
me! Because I haven't told the worst.

I was carrying the princess through an out of the way path. She did-
n't notice that we'd made a detour. I took the lady to the river–bank. I
laid her on the soft grass. I went to get some water from the river. I wet
her face and her neck. She replied with a shiver – that mask of rice
powder was beginning to crack. The princess breathed with difficulty.
She looked around and asked: '*It is si–tation?*'

I decided to lie. I told her it was right there, on the side. We were
by the shade only to hide from the other people who were waiting on
the station platform.

'They mustn't see us. It's better to wait for the train from this hid-
ing–place.'

The poor woman, she thanked me for all my concern. She said
she'd never known a man with such goodness in him. She asked me to
wake her up when it was time; she was very tired, she needed to rest. I
continued to look at her and to feel the nearness of her presence. I saw
the buttons of her dress. I could imagine what sort of fire lay beneath
them. My blood was running fast. At the same time I was tormented
by fear. What if the Master caught me in the middle of the grass with
his lady? There was only one thing: he'd aim the black muzzle of his
gun and shoot. It was the fear of being gunned down that put a stop to
me. I took too long. I was just looking at the woman on my lap. That
was when the dream began to run away from me once again. D'you
know what I felt, Father? It felt as if she didn't have her own body: she
was using mine. D'you understand, Father? That white skin of hers
was mine, that mouth was mine, both those blue eyes were mine. It was
like we were one soul distributed between two opposite bodies; male
and female; one black, one white. You're not convinced? But you
should know this, Father: it's opposites that are always the most similar to each other. You don't believe me. Look: isn't fire that's most similar to ice? They both burn and it is only through death that man can
walk inside the fire and the ice.

But if I was her, then my second body was dying. That's why I felt
so weak. I had given up. I fell down on her side. Neither of us moved.
She had her eyes closed. I was trying to avoid falling asleep. I knew that
if I closed my eyes I would never wake up again. I was too much inside
this; I couldn't afford to go further down. There are times when we
become very similar to the dead and that's what gives the dead their
strength. That's what they don't forgive in us: it's what we, the living

ones, are so similar to them.

And d'you know how I saved myself, Father? I put my hands in the hot ground, like those dying miners had. My roots connected me again with life. That's what saved me. I got up. I was sweating. I had a temperature. I decided to get out of there at once. The princess was still alive and she motioned me to stop. I didn't pay attention. I went back home with the same tightness in my heart that I'd had when I abandoned the survivors on the mine.

When I got there I told the Master that I'd found Milady dead by a tree near the station. I went with him so he'd see I was telling the truth. The princess in the shade could still breathe. When the Master leaned down she held his arms and said: 'Anton!'

The Master heard that name which wasn't his. Even so, he kissed her on the forehead – in a way which showed he cared. I went to fetch the wagon and when we lifted her up she was already dead – as cold as all non–living things. A letter fell from her dress. I tried to catch it but the Master was quicker. He looked at the envelope with surprise and then peered into my face. I had my chin down. I was worried in case he asked. But the Master crumpled up the envelope and put it in his pocket. We returned home in silence.

I ran away to Gondola the next day. I've been there ever since – working for the railways. Now and then I come to Manica and stop by at the old cemetery. I kneel in front of Milady's grave and tell her I'm sorry, what for I don't know. No, actually I do know. I ask her to forgive me for not being the man she was waiting for. But that's all pretending. Father, you know how my kneeling here is all a lie. Because, you see, when I'm standing in front of her grave I can only remember the taste of her body, That's why I'm confessing to this bitterness that has taken away my love for life. There's not much time to go before I have to leave this world. I've already asked God for permission to die. But it looks like God doesn't pay much attention to those kinds of requests. What d'you say, Father? I shouldn't talk like this. Like I'd given up all hope. That's how I remember myself, a widower of a woman whom I never had.

I feel so insignificant now. D'you know what's the only thing that brings joy to my heart? It's when I leave the cemetery and go walking in the dust and the ashes of that mine of those Russians. The mine's closed. It closed down when Milady died. I walk there all alone.

Then I sit on an old trunk and look at the back of me so I can see the tracks I've left behind. And d'you know what I see? I see two kinds of tracks, but both of them made by my own body. Some are of a big foot, a masculine foot. The others are footprints from a small foot, a lady's. They're footsteps of the princess, the one who walks by my side. They're her footsteps, father. That's the one thing I'm dead certain of. Not even God can change this certainty I have. Maybe God won't forgive any of my sins and maybe I'll be in for hell–fire. But I don't care. I'll see her footsteps there, in the ashes of Hell. They'll be walking on my left side.

❋

Caramel Rose

Translated from the Portuguese by Luis Rafael

Not much was known about her. She was known as the hunch-back ever since she was a girl. We called her Caramel Rose. She was one of those upon whom another name is always bestowed. The one she had, the real one, just didn't do. If she was to live in the world it was more apt for her to be baptised again. And we didn't even want to accept something that sounded similar. She was Rose. Subtitle: Caramel. And we laughed.

Hunchback was a mixture of races, her body was the cross–breeding of many continents. As soon as she was ready for life her family left her. The place where she had slept since then wasn't much to look at. It was a hovel made of irregularly shaped boulders, with neither design nor proper height. Inside it not even the wood had evolved to the form of the plank: there was only the trunk, pure matter. Without bed or table the hunchback wasn't one to wait upon herself. Did she eat? No one had ever seen her with any sustenance. Even the eyes were meager from that gauntness of wishing that one day they would be gazed at, with that rounded tiredness of having dreamt.

Her face, nevertheless, was pretty. Taken away from the body, it was even capable of kindling our desires. But if one looked at her from behind, and saw her in her fullness, such prettiness immediately ceased to exist. We saw her wandering on sidewalks, with her short, shuffling steps. In the parks she would keep herself busy: she spoke to the statues. The worst was when she spoke to them of the sicknesses she suffered from. Everything else she did was clouded in silent secrecy, neither seen nor heard. But to exchange words with statues, not that, it was unacceptable. Because the spirit that went into conversations was enough to frighten one. Did she want to cure the scar of the stones? With a motherly instinct she consoled each of the statues:

"Allow me, I'll clean you. I'm going to take away that dirt, it's their dirt."

And she wiped the masonry bodies with a towel, filthy with dirt. Then she returned to the side–paths, now and then allowing herself to be guided by the circle of light shining from the lamp–posts.

During the day we forgot her existence. But at night the light of the moon confirmed for us the crookedness of her shape. The moon seemed to be stuck to the hunchback, like a coin in the hands of a miser. And, facing the statues, she sang in a hoarse and inhuman voice: she asked that they walk out of the stone. She overdreamt.

On Sundays she would retire, a nobody. The old woman disappeared, envious of those who filled the park, staining the restfulness of her territory.

Ultimately one didn't look for an answer to explain Caramel Rose. Only one motive could be reckoned with: at a certain time Rose had waited in suspense, flowers in her hand, at the entrance of the church. The bridegroom, the one that had been, was delayed. He was delayed for so long that he never arrived. He was the one who offered the suggestion: I don't want ceremony. You and I go, only the two of us. Witnesses? Only God, if he's free. And Rose implored:

"But what about my dream?"

All through her life she had dreamt of the wedding feast. A dream of splendour, of a retinue and guests. A moment that would be hers alone, she a queen, beautiful in the envy that spread all around her. With a long white dress, the outline of her back being corrected by a veil. Outside, a thousand hooters. And now, the fantasy was denied to her by the groom. If she could stop crying, to what avail would be loud presentations? She accepted. It would be done his way.

The hour came, the hour went. He neither came nor arrived. The curious onlookers drifted away, taking with them the laughter, the jeers. She waited, waited. No one had ever waited for so long. Only she had, Caramel Rose. She remained on the steps, as if they offered some consolation, reassurance, as if the stone sustained her universal disillusionment.

Stories people tell. Is there a grain of truth in them? It seems that there wasn't ever any bridegroom. She had got all that from her illusions. She had made herself bride. Rosie–the–courted, Rose–the–wed. But if nothing had happened, the outcome was hurtful enough. She had crippled herself for no good reason. To heal the ideas in her head they hospitalised her. But once they put her in hospital they didn't want to know her. Rose didn't get visitors, she never received the medicine of human fellowship. It suited her to be alone, away from people. She made herself sister to the stones, from leaning against them so often. Walls, floor, ceiling: only the stone gave her worth. Rosa laid herself, with the lightness of those who are in love, on the cold flooring. The stone, her twin.

On her discharge the hunchback went in search of her granite soul. It was then that she courted the solitary, reposeful statues. She gave them to drink (when they were thirsty), she protected them on rainy days, when it was cold. Her statue, the favoured one, was the one in the small park in front of our house. It was a monument to some colonial hero, the name of which wasn't even legible. Rose frittered away her time in contemplation of the bust. Love of no return: the man in the form of a statue always remained distant, never condescending to cast his gaze on the hunchback.

Sitting in our verandah, under the zinc roof of our wooden house, we would see her. My father, above all, would see her. He became speechless. Was it the madness of the hunchback that made us lose our reason? My uncle joked about and so saved the day:

"She's like the scorpion. She carries the poison on her back."

We shared the laughter amongst ourselves. All of us, except for my father. He was completely left out, serious.

"No one sees her tiredness. Always carrying her back on her back."

My father was much troubled by the sight of strange forms of weariness. He wasn't one to exhaust himself. Seated, he helped himself to many of life's calm moments. My uncle, a resourceful man, warned him:

"Brother Juca, find yourself some way of living."

My father didn't even reply. It really looked as though he'd become, himself, leaned back, an accomplice of the old chair. Our uncle was right: he needed a salaried job. His only diligence was hiring out his own shoes. On Sunday his friends from the club stopped by on the way to the soccer match.

"Juca, we came 'cause of the shoes."

He nodded, with extreme slowness.

"You know the deal: you take them and then, when you come back, you tell me how the game went."

He bowed down to remove the shoes under the chair. He lowered himself with such effort it looked as though he was trying to catch the very floor. He lifted the pair of shoes and feigned a goodbye as he looked at them:

"It's really hard on me."

He only stayed at home because of the doctor. Too much strain on the heart, on the flow of the blood, had been forbidden to him.

"Rubbish heart."

He beat at his breast to punish the organ. He then turned to the shoes, and chatted to them:

"Watch well, my little shoes: at the right time you come back home."

And he received the money, in advance. He counted the money, slowly, with drawn–out gestures. It was as if he were reading a fat book, one of those that favour the fingers more than the eyes.

My mother: she was the one that stepped out into the world. She was out early in the morning, on her way. The morning was still young when she got to the market. The world was barely visible during the early morning rehearsal of the sun. Mother cleaned her stand before the other sellers did. Behind the heaps of cabbages was her face, a fat face of many sad silences. There she sat, both her and her body. In life's struggle mama had somehow eluded us. She arrived and she left in the dark. At night we heard her, scolding father's laziness.

"Juca, do you think about life?"

"I think much about life."

"Sitting down?"

My father's replies were sparse. She, and only she, complained:

"I am alone, I work inside, I work outside."

Bit by bit, the voices in the corridor die down. My mother still uttered a few sighs, swoons of hope. But we never blamed our father. He was a good man. So good that he could never defend himself.

And life in our small district continued very much the same. Until one day we received the news: Caramel Rose had been arrested. Her only offence: the veneration of a colonialist. The head of the militia ascribed the sentence to: longing for the past. The madness of the hunchback was merely the cover for other, political, reasons. So said the commander. If it wasn't that, what other motive would she have in opposing, with violence, with her whole body, the demolishing of the statue? Yes, because that monument was a foot from the past leaving its tracks in the present time. For respect for the nation to be preserved it was necessary to press for the decapitation of the statue.

So they took old Rose away, so they could cure these alleged thoughts of hers. It was only then, in her absence, we saw how much she filled our landscape.

For a long time we heard no news. Until one afternoon my uncle broke the silence. He had come from the graveyard, from the burial of Jawane, the male nurse. He climbed the small steps of the verandah, interrupting my father's rest. Scratching his legs, my old man blinked his eyes, gauging the amount of light:

"And so, did you bring the shoes?"

My uncle didn't answer at first. He was making use of the shade, relieving himself of the sweat. He blew air into his very lips, tired. In his face I could see the relief of someone who has returned from a funeral.

"Here they are, brand new. Gee man, Juca, these black shoes were really useful!"

He searched his pockets, but the money, always quick to get in, took a long time to come out. My father saved him from further searches:

"To you I didn't hire them. We're family, we wear them together."

My uncle sat down. He poured a bottle of beer into a big glass. Then, with great skill, he took a wooden spoon and with it removed the foam, placing it in another glass. My father took this glass, the one only with foam. Liquids being forbidden to him, the old man devoted himself to the foamy.

"It's so light, this foaminess. The heart doesn't even feel it going through."

He consoled himself, his eyes steady, as if he wished to lengthen the thought. They were no more than a fake, those reflections.

"Were there lots of people at the burial?"

While untying the shoes, my uncle described the throng of people, the crowds trampling over the flower beds, all of them saying farewell to the nurse; poor man, he had himself died.

"But did he really kill himself?"

"Yeah, the guy hanged himself. When they found him he was hard already, as if he was starched hanging from the rope."

"But he killed himself for what reason?"

"Who knows. They say it was because of women."

The two of them were quiet, sipping from their glasses. What hurt them the most was not the fact of the death but the motive for it.

"To die like that? It's better to pass away."

My old man received the shoes and surveyed them distrustfully:

"This sand comes from there?"

"Where's it, that there?"

"I'm asking if it comes from the graveyard."

"Maybe it comes."

"Then go clean it. I don't want the dust of the dead here."

My uncle walked down the steps and sat on the last one, brushing the soles of the shoes. In the meantime he went on telling the story. The ceremony was still going on, the priest said the prayers, blessing the souls with them. All of a sudden, what happens? There arrives Caramel Rose, all dressed up in mourning black.

"Has Rose already left prison?" asked my father (in a voice without tone).

Yes, she had. During an inspection of the prison she had been granted amnesty. She was mad, she wasn't guilty of any serious crime. My father pressed for more, astonished:

"But her, in the cemetery?"

My uncle continued with the account. Rose, from her back down, all in black. Not even a raven, Juca. She went in, spying the graves as if she were a grave–digger. It looked as if she was choosing her own hole. You know, Juca, in the cemetery no one spends much time checking out the excavations. We do it quickly. But this hunchback, she...

"Tell me the rest," cut in my father.

The story went on: standing there, Rose started singing in front of everybody. The mourners just stared at her, bewildered. The priest was still praying, but no one paid any attention to him any more. It was then that the hunchback started undressing.

"You lie, brother."

"True's God, Juca, two thousand knives will fall on me if I lie." She undressed. She started removing her clothes, more slowly than the heat of the day. No one laughed, no one coughed, nobody nothing. When she was naked, without any clothes, she moved close to Jawane's grave. She lifted her arms and threw the clothes over the hole. The sight made the mourners take fright, and they took a few steps back. Rose then prayed:

"Take these clothes, Jawane, you'll need them. Because you're going to be stone like all the others."

Looking at the spectators, she raised her voice, a voice higher than that of any living creature:

"And now: am I allowed to like?"

The mourners retreated, and only the voice of dust spoke to them.

"Not so? I can like this dead one! He's not in time any more. Or is this one also forbidden to me?"

My father rose from his chair; he was almost offended.

"Did Rose speak like that?"

"It's genuine."

And my uncle, ready already, copied the hunchback, her squint body: and this one, can I love him? But my old man would not listen.

"Stop, I won't hear any more."

He spoke so brusquely that his glass fell out of his hands into the air. He wanted to pour out the foam but because of an unfortunate slip the whole thing fell. And as if he were apologising, my uncle picked up the small shards of glass, tumbled upside down throughout the yard.

That night I was unable to sleep. I got out of the house, trying to give the insomnia a rest in the park. I looked at the statue; it had been removed from the pedestal. The colonial had his beard on the ground, and it looked as if he had himself climbed down, so tired of it all. They had pulled down the monument but had forgotten to remove it; the work needed some finishing off. I almost felt sorry for the bearded man, made dirty by the pigeons, covered with dust. Then I switched on, I came to my senses: I'm like Rose, putting feelings into boulders? It was then that I saw Caramel herself, as if my conjuring had beckoned her. I almost froze, unable to move. I wanted to run away, but my legs wouldn't take me. I shuddered: I was becoming a statue, I was turning into the object of the hunchback's affections? Horror, I would never speak again. But, no. Rose didn't stop in the park. She crossed the seat and moved towards the little steps of our house. She lowered herself towards the steps and cleaned the moonlight that shone on them. All her life seemed to dwell in a single sigh. She then huddled herself like a turtle, preparing herself, who knows what for, sleepiness. Or perhaps her only resolve was to feel sadness. For I heard her crying, the murmur of dark waters. The hunchback wept; it looked like her turn to become a statue. A boundless countenance.

It was then my father, with an afflicting silence, opened the door of the verandah. Slowly, he approached the hunchback. For a while he leaned over the woman. Then moving his hand, in the gesture of something long dreamt of, he stroked her hair. In the beginning Rose didn't even move. But, later, she began crawling out of herself, half her face in the light. They gazed at each other, gaining a particular beauty. He then whispered:

"Don't cry, Rose."

I almost didn't hear, my heart leapt up to my ears. I moved closer, always behind the darkness. My father still spoke to her, a kind of voice I had never heard before.

"It's me, Rose. You don't remember?"

I was right in the middle of the bougainvillaea, its thorns tore at me. I didn't even feel them. The dismay jabbed harder than the branches. The hands of my father were drowning in the hunchback's hair, they looked like people, those hands, like people drowning.

"It's me, Juca. Your bridegroom, don't you remember?"

Bit by bit Caramel Rose came to her senses. Never had she felt so intensely about life, no statue had ever deserved such a gaze from her eyes. His voice ever more sweet, my father called out:

"Let's go, Rose."

Effortless, I walked away from the bougainvillaea. They could see me, it wouldn't embarrass me. When the hunchback rose it was as if the light of the moon had been roused.

"Let's go, Rose. Pick up your things, let's go away."

And the two of them went, walking into the night.

Nuruddin Farah

※

The Affair

For Charlie Sugnet

We had known each other for years, she and I. Or did we?
I would call her whenever I was in London, to give her my latest
news. She talked invariably of a husband I had never met, she spoke of
a daughter who had embarked on her monthly interruptions, or alluded to a teenage son who had broken an arm, or been up to some mis-
chief. I would tell her whatever I had done since our last telephone
conversation. Before I rang off, for it was always I who originated the
calls, we would arrange to meet. We knew nothing would come of these
arrangements, even though for some seven years we went through the
motions of fixing appointments neither of us kept. Maybe arranging to
meet gave our telephone conversations a meaning, I have no idea. Even
so, neither reminded the other that we had met only once and that, too,
so very long ago. We might have forgotten both the date and occasion
of our encounter if a brochure prepared for my lecture which I deliv-
ered that evening had not existed. She had offered me a lift to my hotel,
and we talked in the car until it was too late for her to come up to my
room for a nightcap. At some point she referred to a husband waiting
impatiently for her return. I promised I would get in touch with her
again when I was in London. The following morning I left for another
city, I forget which now, and before the month ended I wrote her a
postcard, with no address on it. I was transiting through Rome's
Fiumicino, but didn't give her any details. However, I promised I
would call her up for a chat when I was in England.
    Of one thing I was certain: she was older than I. I was in my early
thirties, she in her middle forties. She had a daughter who had begun
to think of herself as a young woman and behaved as such, and a boy
who was taking his A-levels. There may have been a third child, but I
am not sure. Her husband, I now recall, had been the principal of a col-
lege she had taught at. I also remember being invited by her to their
home so I could meet her entire family. But I was averse to the idea and
so declined the invitation, preferring to keeping a secret line of com-

munication open between her and myself. I feared I might not want to continue nurturing our furtive contact if I had met her husband and children. Mark you, I was not always clear in my mind if I wished to sleep with her, no. As a general rule, I avoid married women. Moreover, I sleep with women either on our second or third encounter, or I never sleep with them at all. So whenever she invited me to her home, I kept declining. Likewise, she would promise to meet me alone in London, but somehow this did not appear to happen.

Now and then I dreamt lovingly about her, many of my dreams ending in dampness. But I never told her about my dreams when we spoke on the telephone. Nor did I tell her how much I wished she and I would have a meal alone by candlelight, as I watched her hazel eyes in the dimly lit hotel room, my foot teasing her stockinged leg. I imagined a rushed scene of love-making, imagined her consulting her watch frequently, and speaking of her husband or children needing her to look after them. I hoped that, upon leaving me, she would ache for me as she swung corners, reached the blind curves, which she took in her embrace, and she would longingly think about me and of the brief love we had shared. My name, I hoped, would for ever remain an initial in her diary, a mysterious letter never to grow the flesh one associates with a name consisting of vowels and consonants and of the physicalness of a pronounceable name.

Let me add this: I have a weakness. I respond positively to women older, and in their own way, wiser then I. I think it wonderful to have a female companion capable of filling my days with stimulating discussions. Encountering these women produces in me such lusty feelings that, having been turned on, I then try to make an earthy contact of a corporeal kind.

I do not recall her name. But then I seldom needed to call her by name. After all, she knew my voice, which, as she put it, had in it a touch of sand, maybe because I come from the semi-arid northern reaches of the Somali peninsula. Besides, I called her when her husband was at work and her son and daughter were likely to be away from home. Only once did the husband answer. I cut off the communication, explaining, "Wrong number, sorry!" and hung up. As for her when she picked it up, she was quick enough to sense the earthy huskiness of my voice: and she would take over and speak and speak and speak. Then she would fall silent abruptly, put a few questions to me and give me a couple of minutes to deal with them while she waited impatiently to talk. I would tell her my latest news, where I had been, what I had done with my time. I loved to hear her voice, loved to listen to her theories, of which she had legion. I believed that her head burst with the wealthy propensity of so many first-time-heard theories, and that I was of some service to her, she who was as capable of arguing about a philosophical point as she was of wiping away the drool on a teething baby's chin, but who hadn't a husband loving enough to listen to her. In the Africa you come from, she would say, paraphrasing Saint-Exupery(accent on e), ".....intellectuals are kept in reserve on the shelves of the Ministry of Propaganda, like pots of jam to be eaten when the famine is over". One day I lost my reserve and made a flippant remark: how women like her ought not to mind pots and babies, but should attend to the turn of the wind in their minds, or should follow the mirage of their elusive selves. "You ought to be free," I concluded, "to breed thoughts, not only babies." Vexed, I had no idea why, she hung up on me.

I called her up the following morning. And neither alluded to what transpired between us the day before. As though emboldened by this, I suggested that she and I spend a few days together in total isolation, "days whose suns might brighten the smile in her eyes, and nights whose moon might moisten the runny darkness of her mascara". She was discomfited by the changes in my attitude towards our relationship, making it clear that she didn't like the direction I was headed. I remarked a change in us both. I hung up, a little vexed, without promising to ring her up during my next visit to London. She did not augur me well in my travels, a departure from her usual farewell warm wishes. Something had taken place, but what?

When next in London I called her from Heathrow to inform her that I was going to be in the city for a week. Did she have the time to meet up? I had never known her to speak briefly and to the point, but that was what she did. I should've prepared myself for more surprises in store for me, but I didn't. Saying that her husband and children had gone off for a few days to Wales, she wondered would we have a candlelit dinner as I had often intimated? I gave her the address of where I was putting up.

You would think she had been starved, the clumsy way she ate fast, breathing, panting as she took mouthfuls of the food, on occasion knocking the candles over. You would think she was insane, the inordinate noises she emitted when we made love. Why was she in such haste? Was she getting things out of the way? Why couldn't she wait for me, a slow eater, to finish my meal? Why did she not show the slightest interest in talking the excitingly intelligent way she had often talked to me on the phone? I had looked forward to her coming, and had asked for room service, no expenses spared. There was a bouquet of roses, there was my gift to her too. I am inclined to be romantic and like being seduced first by the forcefulness of the woman's intelligence before I am gradually persuaded by the eloquence of a shared emotion. But that was not to be.

Her clumsiness knew no bounds, her noise recognised no limits! I wondered if anyone in the corridor might hear us. She was mechanical, she was methodical in the manner of air hostesses, too forward and too brusque for my taste. In a matter of some ten minutes, we made love twice. The first time I pretended as if I enjoyed every instant, but couldn't help betraying my unease when she went down for a second go soon after the first disaster. I caught her looking up at me, as though her hazel eyes were questioning my slackness. I chose to ignore the questions now invading my mind, and decided to shut these self-queries off in the same way as you shut off a terrible *colpo d'aria*.

Undeterred in her desire to please, she suggested we run a bath, soap each other's back, play footsie and see. I consented. Once in the bathtub together, I kept changing the subject, leading our conversation back to a real talk between two intelligent persons. I lay back in the tub, across from where she was, and was as formal as a Chinaman. For a while I thought she had regained the grace I associated with her in my mind when she spoke of the war. She had been in her teens then, and had taken an aversion to a brand of chocolate available in England in those days. Presently she stood up and, not bothering to explain, stepped out of the bath. I followed suit.

When next I stood close to her, she smelt of some French perfume sprayed as though at the wake of a disastrous moment. She sat in one of the chairs nearer the bed, looking uncomfortable. She smiled awkwardly, her eyes betraying a certain antagonism. Neither of us spoke for a quarter of an hour.

"You think I've been cheap, don't you?" she said.

I didn't speak, but waited uncomfortably, considering the implications of her remark.

"You think I've been as cheap as a whore, don't you?" she charged.

I didn't know what to say. No, let me rephrase it: I didn't know how to express the sad thoughts which had come to my mind. Fearful that she might accuse me of imposing my will upon her, I recoiled, recalling how often women were heard to advise that before engaging in love, it was best that the couple knew each other better. Men were supposed to be impatient, when it came to love-making, because they grew lustily hot where women remained cool and placid. No doubt things do not make sense when spoken in the heat of coupling, when one is wet in the groin, when one might tell any lie to arrive at a sexual truth. Before today, I had believed that women's self-restraint was greater than a man's, that they were ultimately more capable of touching the origin of their own otherness: men, who blew hot where women blew cold! In short, I was taken aback by her total abandonment of sexual protocol.

"What does that make you, if you think that I am as cheap as a whore!" she said.

I went closer to her, toweringly tall, my posture suggestive of a man unprepared to be judged by a self-condemned woman. One of her knees was now touching the floor, the other was detained in the knot the edge of the towel had rolled itself into. I had no idea what I was doing, but I extended my hand, maybe in a gesture to make peace. When it became obvious to me that she didn't want us to touch, I said, "It takes two to make love."

I had expected her to point out to me that I was a man, to wit a woman's imagined nightmare, the consequences of her measled fever. This was how she put it when, within the first week of our meeting, she spoke of her husband, whom she likened to a zebra. Take away the stripes, and a zebra is but a donkey! I doubt that I understood what she had meant, only there was something highly imaginative about the way she said these things. Quite often I had replayed portions of our telephone conversations in my mind. Was this to be no more?

Now we were purposelessly silent. To alter our mood, I helped her get to her feet. Whereupon both our towels dropped to the floor. Naked, we held hands for a moment or two, kissed and touched each other here and there. In a moment, and to my relief, I was a rising fibre of muscles, and was overwhelmed with heated lust; she was warm, she was moist. We kissed a little more passionately, her eyes runny with tears, my cheeks stained with their dampness. I dragged her to bed, maybe because I believed we might make things better by overriding the disastrous consequences of the previous few minutes.

She said, "I hardly know you."

"Nonsense!" I said.

"And you hardly know me!"

I insisted, "But I do."

We made love, as though the future of our relationship depended on it. I kissed away her tears, she kissed away the unspoken dots of my misgivings. There was no need for me to worry about her untoward noises, for she made none until the end as she arrived. I stopped her mouth with my hand and she bit deeply into it.

I could not sleep!

She lay on her back, like an upturned wagon, her legs moving every now and then as if they were the wheels of a vehicle someone had jerked into motion. Her snore reminded me of the laboured noise a car makes when its battery is low. I got out of bed, and switched on the lights, maybe because I hoped this would wake her up. I needed a minute or two to fall asleep before she resumed her heavy snoring. No such thing. She lay on her back, dead to my awoken worries. I poked her in the ribs hard and called to her until she was awake. She sat up, startled. She squinted, the bright light hurting her eyes. "What's the matter?" she said.

I said, "You're snoring!"

"Snoring?" she asked, as if she didn't know the meaning of the word. "Me, snoring?"

I nodded my head.

"But I never do," she said. "My husband does. I don't!"

Not knowing what to say to this, I fell silent. Then she apologised: maybe her inner worries were making unprecedented demands on her unconscious. I suggested she give me time to fall asleep myself. She acceded to my request. But no sooner had she turned her back on me than she dropped into her deeply disturbed sleep, still snoring.

The lights off, I moved about the room and busied myself with other thoughts, other errands. I gathered the food plates and left them outside the door for the hotel staff to find them there in the morning. I hung the hotel's Do-not-disturb sign on the door, rummaged in the cupboards for a blanket and a pillow and lay down on the carpeted floor, in the furthest corner from her. I could hear the orchestra of her nostrils, the A- and B-majors in her sinuses.

Now it was she towering above me, and telling me to please wake up.

I did so, wondering if I too had snored.

"I am going," she announced. She was already dressed and ready to leave.

"What time is it?" I asked.

"My husband will be ringing," she told me, "and I want to be home when he does."

From here on the uncertainties begin. Did I fall asleep after she left because I didn't wake up until after midday, on the bed, even though I had no idea how I got there? But then why did it feel as though I had slept alone all along in my hotel bed with me! I've often wondered if I had dreamt it all. Could it be that *she* and I never met a second time, that I had dreamed the love we made, the quarrel we had, the room service meal we ate together? Perhaps I had dreamt about her in the same way I dreamt about her for a very long time, dreams in which we made love. Presently I thought about some psycho-jargons, something to do with epiphanies, with the revenge of the unconscious on the conscious. As I once again drifted into sleep, I heard her voice insisting that I hardly knew her.

America, Her Bra!

On first hearing America alluded to in an intimate way, I fell under the impression that it was the name of a beautiful girl with whom I was sure I would fall in love the instant I laid my eyes on her. The two youths that kept referring to her with knowing grins on their faces had known cities, one of them having visited Mogadiscio, the other having been brought up in Addis Ababa. I had known no place bigger than Kallafo, a farming town in the backwater of the Somali-speaking Ogaden in Ethiopia, where our family had moved when I was barely three. Fascinated I listened to them regale one another with their fantastic find, imagining America to be a tantalizing houri-seductress, who would provide me with an entry into the corrupt world of adulthood.

I was about ten then, and life in our part of the world was changing at a rapid pace. We may not have thought of ourselves as newly reconstructed hicks, but we were all aware that we were living in momentous times, our way of life being altered by forces we could only dimly comprehend. We were abandoning our eating habits, giving up our daily intake of milk- and meat-based diets in exchange for easy-to-prepare meals, like rice, spaghetti and other starch-based dishes. Our vocabulary was enriched daily by new words of foreign derivation, loan words from the Italian or Arabic for garments till then unknown to us, like underpants, socks, and handkerchiefs.

As the youths amused themselves, one of them alluded to maraikaan, a coarse and cheap fabric of cotton imported from America and much admired by Somali nomads. When I saw the garment of which they were speaking, I couldn't at first understand what the excitement was all about. It dawned on me, soon enough, however, that they were not talking about a girl called America but an item of women's clothing, which one of them now held up against the sun, his fingers clutching at either end of it.

From where I stood, I had no idea what use the item might be put to. Even so I could see that the material was intricately joined together. The loops of the cup-shaped garment were thickly padded, and of standard-issue cotton; and much of the sewing was doubly strengthened. It had metal hooks at one end, and eyes at the other. I asked, "What is it?" But neither bothered to answer.

In my memory, I recall the charged expressions on the faces of the youths as they imagined themselves to be in the company of the American woman whose brassiere they held in their hands. One of them, closing his eyes, had imagined himself taking a bucket bath with her and spoke with joy of the water cascading from on high. The other claimed that he slept with the bra under his pillow and was transported every dawn to a land, not of milk and frankincense but of white flesh and fragrant hair.

I viewed the world of the brassiere with ominous foreboding, a double-edged seduction, through which our bodily desires were being refashioned, thanks to our acquisition of these accoutrements of American modernity. We were no longer in control of our bodies ourselves. I thought I knew what one of the youths meant when he claimed that holding the brassiere, stolen from the woman's washing-line, made him feel as though he was journeying to the beyond of the land beyond, where his life would be transformed. Was it because a brassiere is such a high-tech affair that these boys now assumed a posture of sophistication? The two youths started to think of themselves as leagues apart from everyone else in our town, as if calling the bra theirs at last placed them in a separate mental territory.

In Kallafo, the river was a prominent feature, dividing our part of town and the part where the provincial authority was situated, on Government Hill, close to a church-run school and the American compound, where the woman to whom the brassiere belonged lived with her husband. Curious, I braved my way out to the American compound for the first time, a boat that crossed between our side of the river and hers. There I learnt that she was the wife of the school's director. And before the year was out, the two youths were enrolled in the American missionary school as students, and soon after that became the new converts at the chapel.

Lília Momplé

✴

Celina's Banquet

Translated from the Portuguese by Richard Bartlett

Lourenço Marques, April 1950

"It's beautiful," sighs Leonor, examining the dress.

Dona Violante de Sousa doesn't respond, but her face shines with pride as she hangs up the masterpiece which is the product of her hands. She has put the finishing touches to the white organza dress which her daughter Celina will wear to the Salazar High School matriculants' banquet. A hem of perfect lace, running between two ruffles, decorates the neckline and the shoulders. An identical hem, just slightly broader, elegantly finishes off the long gown. It is, actually, a beautiful dress in its apparent simplicity.

"How lucky she is, having a dressmaker for a mother! I'm certain that Celina's dress will be one of the most beautiful!" says Dona Celeste.

The three women are talking in Dona Violante's dining room, which also serves as a sewing room. Leonor is a good–looking mulatto with her thirty years, married to a placid worker on the railways. Throughout her entire married life she has deceived her husband and, about two months ago, ended up abandoning him to become the latest lover of old Sales Moreira, a stinking–rich white man, married and with sons already grown up. Dona Violante has known Leonor since before she was married and, to tell the truth, never appreciated her way of living. She considers her as a loose woman and, were she not a customer, would never receive her in the house. Dona Celeste, also a mulatto, is an old friend of Dona Violante. She suffers from a strange illness which the doctors ascribe to the menopause. And because in Iapala, where her husband lives, medical facilities are virtually non–existent, she has come to Lourenço Marques for treatment. Dona Violante, owner of the house, was born on Mozambique Island, and her history is curiously linked to that of the old millionaire Catarino da Silva, head of one of the greatest fortunes of the colony.

When this man, native of Urgeiriça in Portugal, disembarked on Mozambique Island, he brought with him only his 'face and his courage'. But he also brought, well hidden inside, a strong conviction that Africa existed to make the whites richer and, in a special way, him, Catarino da Silva. So, furnished with such a powerful spiritual weapon, he put his hands to work. He began by going to live with a black girl, the gifted Alima, who roasted peanuts perfectly and, as he discovered much later, with the same peanuts baked delicious torritoris caramel sweets. Catarino da Silva spent his time selling roasted peanuts and torritoris, also taking on himself the job of managing the money from the sales. And he managed it so well that in a short time he could join up with another settler, Benjamim Castelo, owner of the only butcher shop on the island. It is very likely that the nickname Silva Porco, by which he is known in Ponta da Ilha to this day, had something to do with his somewhat unkempt appearance, before he had turned into a rich man.

The partnership of Catarino da Silva–Benjamim Castelo prospered on all fronts, thanks to cheating and the unchecked exploitation of black workers, forcibly rounded up by the colonial authorities. In this way they prospered so that, within a few years, the two partners were owners of enormous plantations of sisal and cotton, machambas and shops spread over almost all of the north of the colony.

At this point Catarino da Silva understood that the time had come to rid himself of his black girlfriend and to make himself a worthwhile marriage. He then cast his greedy eyes on the young Maria Claudina Bordalo Monteiro, renowned all over the island for her beauty and for having passed the fifth year of high school, a notable achievement for a girl in those days. She was the daughter of the lawyer Bordalo Monteiro, member of a ruined Portuguese noble family who, with grown children, had ended up, at his wife's insistence, leaving Portugal and going to Mozambique Island. Not that she had any desire to live on the Island, which she barely knew anyway. What she desired was to leave Portugal, a long way behind if possible, finally to get her husband away from the overbearing influence of his noble parents, confirmed drunkards and cheats, incapable of benefiting her life. At that time fateful circumstances helped the whole family to reach the Island. There is no doubt that the move brought them advantages. In fact, the constant court cases between the shop owners of the Island, mostly the Indians, were an inexhaustible manna for Dr Bordalo Monteiro who got what he wanted, defending causes just and unjust. It is known that he spent a large part of the money he earned gambling the night away. But he always left enough to support the family at a level they would never have reached in Portugal.

Maria Claudina was eighteen years old when Catarino da Silva asked for her hand in marriage. And to everyone's surprise, even slightly to his own, he was accepted. The girl obviously followed the advice of her mother who, after having suffered with her husband's noble family, considered the marriage of her daughter to a man who was simultaneously common and rich beyond measure a true blessing. The wedding was a grand affair. And, equally to everyone's surprise, the couple suited each other perfectly. From the start Maria Claudina knew that her husband saw her above all as a trampoline to position himself in society. For his part Catarino da Silva had no illusions as to the motives which led the girl to accept him, with his grotesque figure, his hillbilly fashion sense and rudimentary education. He knew that he only presented her with the possibility of a future free of economic and emotional pitfalls, the primary objective in the life of a daughter of a man full of failings. Such an absence of romanticism in a marriage can only lead to a complete split or, as happened in this case, a more perfect harmony.

In this way, Catarino da Silva felt fulfilled, as only those who have been able to give shape to their very deepest desires can be fulfilled.

As he had expected, Africa had turned him into a rich man and, because of his wealth, he was also a respected man. And the atmosphere of happiness in which he lived was almost tangible, which did not go by unnoticed with Benjamim Castelo, his partner.

"Castelo," said Catarino da Silva provocatively at times, with badly disguised pride, "you also ought to get married with a girl like Maria Claudina. A man needs to have a family. Forget your black girl, that was only necessary in the beginning."

"But I have a baby girl, Violante. She's still very small and it'll hurt to separate her from her mother," replied the partner.

"Listen, don't separate them. Leave her with her mother, there'll be no shortage of children…and legitimate ones," insisted the other.

At first the idea of abandoning his girlfriend and daughter disgusted Benjamim Castelo. Without ever having taken notice of the fact, he had become attached to Muaziza, her sweet manners, her unique insight and even the fresh smell of her body. He had also become fond of his daughter, a handful of tenderness and grace, to whom he had given the name Violante in memory of his own mother. But, while feeling sentimental, Benjamim Castelo was also easily influenced. And, little by little, he began to desire next to him the presence of a white woman who could receive his friends with the same openness with which Maria Claudina presided over the get–togethers at his partner's house. Finally, he needed someone whom he could consider as his true wife, giving him legitimate children who could associate with other white children.

Without realising it, his gentle moods changed to include a growing impatience which Muaziza bore in stoic silence. In the end he appeared at the house at meal times, ate quickly, his brow creased, speaking only to complain if something irritated him. And at night he threw himself into bed and slept until sunrise, a heavy and unkind sleep, like a drunkard. Even the playfulness of little Violante didn't make him happy. And the child became restrained and shy, which irritated him even further.

One day, on arriving at the house for lunch, he could find neither Muaziza nor his daughter. On the laid table there was his lunch, still hot on serving plates.

"They've gone then," he thought immediately, looking at the plates which, covered like that, seemed an obvious sign of farewell.

He searched for them all over the house, but only the enveloping silence answered, emphasising the sound of his steps. He realised then that Muaziza had taken the only trunk with all the clothes she and her daughter owned. She left neither a message nor an address with the neighbours. Much later Benjamim Castelo found out that the girl had gone to her mother's house in Mossuril. There she lived with Violante, providing for her from what the old woman's small machamba could produce, sometimes barely enough to eat.

When Catarino da Silva found out about Muaziza's flight, he comforted his partner with great outbursts of joy. "Hey man, what good luck that she left," he shouted, dancing with his small skipping steps. "I'd seen that nothing else could set you free from that black woman. She's left, and good for her. Scoundrel that she is, she ought to have realised that it was high time to become scarce. I've better judgement than you with your silly morals, in longing for her now. And what of the little coloured girl: let her be with her mother. I think it's stupid to go looking for her."

"But she's my daughter," interrupted the partner timidly.

"She's your daughter, she's your daughter. I know that, I know she's your daughter," continued the other. "And it's only for her own good that I think it's better for her to stay with her mother. Suppose you had married? Where is the woman who would put up with a mulatto step–daughter? And if you had children? What would it be like with the mulatto girl among white brothers and sisters?"

"That's true, she was trouble," agreed Benjamim Castelo, somewhat perplexed.

"Don't I know she was trouble! No man, don't torment yourself with useless remorse. Forget the little girl, once and for all, it's better for you and for her. If you go looking for her, I guarantee it'll only bring complications in the future," concluded Catarino da Silva, giving his partner a friendly pat on the back.

This conversation laid Benjamim Castelo's doubts to rest and he began to see Muaziza's flight as a release. And with a free conscience, with the precious help of his partner, he set about finding a bride from among the white girls on the island.

The choice fell on the young Maria Adelaide, only daughter of the admiral of the Port Authority. She wasn't quite as brilliant as the wife of Catarino da Silva. But she was a girl of courteous manners and a wholesome and fresh appearance. At the same time she was pleased with her suitor, not only because of his wealth but also because of his calm and gentle manners, the dark complexion of his skin and, above all, by a certain air of helplessness which really appealed to her maternal instinct. They were married, and neither Benjamim Castelo nor his friends informed the girl of the existence of the little Violante. He for fear of offending her, and the others because they didn't think it worth their while.

The first two years of marriage was a succession of happy days. In this way they never became aware of the illness which surreptitiously was laying waste to Benjamim Castelo's healthy body. When they discovered it, they left immediately for Portugal to get better medical facilities, but still nothing could be done. It was then, on his deathbed, moved by belated remorse, that Benjamim Castelo revealed to his wife the existence of little Violante. And, contrary to what he expected, this revelation became a source of hope and a stimulus for his wife to continue living. In reality, as they had no children, that child arose like an extension of her husband, something of his which survived for her to protect and to love.

After the death of her husband, Maria Adelaide wrote a long letter to Catarino da Silva. Mainly it was to inform him that she didn't wish to return to Mozambique. She also asked him to arrange for a share of the estate to be received by herself as the widow of Benjamim Castelo. Finally she urged him to get into contact with Violante's mother and inform her that, as was the express desire of Benjamim Castelo before he died, all the necessary legal requirements for the child to come to enjoy the fruits of all her rights as his daughter would be seen to. Maria Adelaide said she would also like to attend to the education of the youngster, with the mother's agreement, as she continued to be the only holder of maternal power.

Catarino da Silva hurried to answer Maria Adelaide's letter. He told her he was in complete agreement with her staying on in Portugal. He promised to take care of the estate quickly, and effectively did so. But, by bribing the legal officers, he succeeded in robbing the widow in any way he could, and in a very crude manner. Regarding the young Violante, he was quick to respond that such a daughter did not exist, attributing the declaration of his partner to the hallucinations of a man on his deathbed.

Furious, Maria Adelaide didn't write again, deciding rather to handle the subject of the child through legal channels. In this way Muaziza was called to make a statement in court, as it depended on her to confirm that Violante was the daughter of the late Benjamim Castelo. And, to the surprise of even the judge who knew the case, she declared that the child was the daughter of a white sailor who had stayed over on the Island and had never returned.

In this way Violante lost all the rights as heir left to her by Benjamim Castelo. Maria Adelaide never knew the reasons which brought Muaziza to give false testimony. But Muaziza carried with her until her death the anguished memory of that decisive hour in Violante's destiny.

It was in Catarino da Silva's office where she, standing, heard what this one, sitting at his desk, said to her in his 'black Portuguese'. "I am calling you to tell that Castelo died," he began. "His wife wants to take away your daughter for her. She wants go to court and everything. If you want keep your daughter you must tell the court she is not child of Castelo. If you tell that she is child of Castelo, you will never see her again. I am telling you because I have pity, a child so small without mother, going so far with nobody! It is for this that I am telling you. If the court asks…"

And he continued with this advice in a gentle tone, until the words were cast in an obscene mould of complicity.

Muaziza did not stop to wonder at the sudden anxiety on the part of someone who had never wanted to know either her or her child. But she had nobody else who could explain the complicated and terrible laws of the whites. And the panic at losing her daughter for ever led her to follow the advice which Catarino da Silva had given. Only much later did she understand his real intentions.

At that time Violante was eight years old. But she had already experienced the insecurity, the fears, the violent contradictions inherent in her situation as a colonised mulatto. And the suffering which this situation caused her became almost unbearable with the passing of the years. Because of this, when Celina, her only daughter, was born, she promised herself to defend her, at all costs, from the humiliations which lay in wait through the sole fact of being mulatto. And she attempted to keep that promise, adopting a strategy which seemed more than adequate for her intentions. In reality, this strategy was limited to providing her daughter with the best education because, in her opinion, this was the only way of guaranteeing at least acceptance on the part of the master of the land, in other words, the settlers. How far she could go with such conviction not even she could guess, perhaps from the fact of not knowing a single mulatto with a level of education beyond primary.

Aware that the education of a child is a costly venture, Dona Violante turned her hands to her gift of making clothes, spending nights on end sewing for other people, in the end adding a little money to the meager salary of her husband. When Celina had reached her seventh year she was enrolled in the Luis de Camoens School, the only one on the Island. From then on, because bad pronunciation of Portuguese was sufficient reason to fail an exam, the child was expressly forbidden by her mother from speaking Macua, a language she had mastered with fluency and love. She also observed a rigorous study timetable. In this way, not being an especially gifted child, thanks to the iron–willed discipline imposed on her, she completed her primary education with some success.

Inspired by the good results achieved by her daughter, and because the only high school in the colony was to be found in Lourenco Marques, Dona Violante persuaded her husband to ask for a transfer so that Celina could continue with her studies. It was not easy for a poor man, a lowly third–class artisan, to obtain the longed for transfer. And so it was granted only after two successive years of whining and humble petitions and requests. The family then did move to Lourenco Marques, and Celina was finally able to enroll at Salazar High School.

Established to serve the interests of the settlers, the high school clearly reflects the racial segregation prevailing in Mozambique. In her final year Celina and a young Indian are the only students of colour, and in the whole school there is not a single black student. During the first years, in that atmosphere, Celina only wanted to pass by unnoticed. But, just the same, she was often to read in the expressions of most of her colleagues and teachers the interrogation: "But what is that mulatto girl doing here? Does she not know this isn't her place?"

Meanwhile, the habit of disciplined study weighed in her favour. Actually, despite usually being unjustly criticised as a result of the colour of her skin, Celina has always been a good student. And this fact has won her, little by little, some acceptance on the part of her colleagues. So, inspired by this unexpected gift, today she is capable of laughing, talking and even presenting a façade of being accepted at will in the presence of other students of the high school. Despite this she doesn't ignore the fact that this acceptance which they show has its limits. And it's not possible to step over this limit without a gesture, a word or a sudden silence to remind her of the colour of her skin.

Meanwhile Dona Violante frets on in her happiness, glued day and night to her sewing machine so that there is no shortage of money for fees, books and clothes for her daughter. And when at times Celina laments the contempt or indifference of her fellow students, her mother responds in a voice of unshakable confidence: "Study, girl! Only education can obliterate our colour. The more you study, the faster you become human!"

And now, looking once again at the gown which Celina will wear to the matric banquet, she sees a partial affirmation of her words. In fact, the matric banquet of Salazar High School is considered to be the major social event of the year in Lourenço Marques. Apart from the teachers, students and their families, only the highest members of colonial society are admitted to the hall, to be honoured with the presence of the very Governor General. Despite all this, Dona Violante thinks, she, her husband and her daughter – simple mulattos – will be there thanks to Celina having reached the seventh year of secondary school.

As if echoing her thoughts, Dona Celeste comments: "Oh, what a thing education is. How could Violante ever have dreamt of one day going to the banquet at Salazar High School! But how your daughter has succeeded..."

"Are you also going?" interrupts Leonor, eyes shining with excitement. "Show us the dress you're going to wear, come on, let's see!"

Dona Violante goes to the room to fetch the dress of black crepe, very sober, its only touch of colour being a long lilac shawl which goes with it.

"You won't be behind those whites," says Leonor, looking at it approvingly.

"All that sacrifice was worthwhile," agrees Dona Celeste eagerly.

And, in agreeing, she includes the exhausting work, nights without sleep and all the hardships her friend had put herself through for Celina to be able to study.

"The sacrifices have not ended yet," replies Dona Violante with pride. "If Celina passes, she's going to continue her studies. Now that she's come this far…"

"How will she continue her studies if Mozambique doesn't have a university?" asks Dona Celeste.

"She'll go to Portugal. Now that she's come this far, she'll go the whole way," concludes Dona Violante, turning to take the dress back to the room.

The other two women cannot find the words to express their admiration for such a spirit of sacrifice.

"Is it true that the Governor also goes to the banquet?" asks Leonor a little later, returning to the topic of the banquet, having an infinite interest in it.

"He goes every year," says Dona Violante, with all the assurance of a mother of a matriculant.

At that point the three begin commenting on the personal life of the Governor General: a lazy and poisonous man, distinguished only by his unrestrained passion for horses and beautiful mulatto women. He even sends for lovers in his official car and then, obviously, lets them come in at the back entrance of Ponta Vermelha Mansion.

"I pity his wife," says Dona Violante, pursing her lips. "He could at least deceive her with other white women. But with women of an inferior race, that takes the cake."

Dona Celeste and Leonor obviously agree, as they are also convinced of the inferiority of their own kind, even if as in Leonor's case this is only a pretence as she has seduced the husbands of many a white woman. And their commentary only ends when, already close to lunch–time, both of them leave, wishing Dona Violante the greatest success at the banquet.

"Like Celina you ought to be happy," says Leonor on her way out.

Meanwhile Celina is busy in the majestic hall of the high school and is not as happy as all that. She is now a good–looking young woman with all the vigour of her twenty years. She commands unusual charm and the features so marked in mulatto women. Yet she is not beautiful, due to a strange expression in her eyes, simultaneously distrustful, hard and passive. Eyes which reflect uneasiness of spirit and, because of this, are unpleasant to look at.

While the shouts and bursts of laughter of the final year students fill the large space where the banquet will take place, Celina tries to get involved in the lively atmosphere felt on the eve of the great event. Nevertheless, as always when she is among her fellow students, she feels tormented and has the acute sensation of her outward appearance being false and too happy, leaving a bitter taste deep inside her. She concentrates on her job of arranging flowers to decorate the hall. Aware of the absolutely farcical role she plays in this situation, with great astonishment she hears her name in a loud bellow: "Student Celina de Sousa and Student Jorge Vieira are called to the headmaster's office!" shouts one of the teachers who has just entered the hall.

A sudden silence follows the words of the teacher who, irritated that nobody is responding, repeats himself in a very serious and offended tone. Only then does Celina put down the flowers she is arranging and, trembling inside, go to the teacher. Now the fright has given way to panic, because the headmaster sees fit to call up students only in very serious cases. And the fact that Jorge Vieira, the only student of colour besides herself, is also summonsed, does not bode well. Scared to death and a little embarrassed, both of them follow the teacher, leaving behind them a murmur of curiosity.

"The students you wanted to see are here, sir!" announces the teacher respectfully, ushering them into the headmaster's office.

The headmaster is seated at his desk and responds with a curt nod of his head. He is a dry and thin man, with the air of someone who is always bored with the things and people around him. He seems so distant and so absorbed in what he is writing that, for a moment, Celina doubts that he has really called for them.

"We need to talk," says the headmaster at last, putting his pen on the blotting pad.

Celina and her fellow student stand in front of his desk, not daring to look at one another.

"I want to tell you that you cannot go to the matric banquet," continues the headmaster calmly, resting his short–sighted vision on the students.

Celina cannot believe what she is hearing. Her temples throb and an uncontrollable nausea numbs her feelings. She remains standing with difficulty, hearing the voice of the headmaster which sounds so gentle, so distant...

"Undoubtedly you understand," he continues. "There are certain unpleasant things I need to do from time to time. The Governor General himself is coming, as are people who are not used to socialising with people of colour. And you will also not have wanted to sit and chat in their midst! To avoid irritation on all sides, we thought it better if you did not come to the banquet. It would be very annoying if…"

Celina and her fellow do not dare answer back, crushed by that calm voice, distant, full of authority. They both wish the headmaster would finish his monologue and let them leave.

"You may go," he orders finally, returning immediately to his writing.

At the same time, in Celina's house, Dona Violante and her husband are having lunch, talking nervously about the banquet the next day, to which they are looking forward with a mixture of pride and apprehension. The absence of their daughter doesn't bother them. She told them she would probably arrive much later because of preparations for the banquet. Anyway, it would take a great deal for them to imagine that, while they are having lunch, the girl is wandering the streets, trying to gather the courage to face them and repeat what the headmaster has said to her. Besides, since that declaration, in a soft and distant voice, that she could not go to the matric banquet, Celina has been wandering in a semi–conscious nightmare. After leaving the headmaster's office she did not return to the majestic hall. She left the high school quickly and walked aimlessly down the streets. And when, tired and lightly feverish, she finally returns home, her father has already left for work and her mother is resting in her bedroom.

When, much later, Dona Violante goes again to work in the sewing room, it takes a while before she notices that Celina's gown, which she had left hanging up, is gone. Smiling to herself, she goes to the little room where her daughter sleeps, as she thinks Celina has taken the gown, perhaps to admire it better.

But what she sees on opening the door leaves her dumb with fright and indignation. Sitting on her bed with a pair of scissors, Celina is cutting up her beautiful white gown.

"Are you mad?!" shouts her mother, recovering from the first moments of shock.

Celina doesn't answer, doesn't even raise her eyes. Calmly, determined, she continues to slice the dress into little pieces which are strewn on the floor like fragile and vaporous clouds, scattered by the breeze.

✳

An Event in Saua-Saua

Translated from the Portuguese by Richard Bartlett

June 1935

Mussa Racua slowly approaches the hut of Abudo. All the tired-ness of an entire day of fruitless wandering is concentrated in his melancholic serene gaze which reflects a sadness with no hope. Now slow, his walk does not hint at the energy spent since dawn, cross-ing great distances between the huts of friends and acquaintances without rest. A walk with firm steps, with head raised, his tall and slen-der body stands tall. He knows how to keep the anxiety and grief burn-ing inside him hidden. Only his eyes, far too serene, far too staring, give an inkling of the weariness of a player who has lost everything.

Abudo is his last hope. Nevertheless, a hope so remote and fleeting that, far from animating him, it fills him with fear. The only reason he does not turn back is to prove that he has fought to the end.

As he had expected, his friend receives him resting his back against the small blue door of his hut.

"Good afternoon brother," greets the newly arrived.

"Good afternoon," replies Abudo.

They grasp hands in the manner of the coastal Macua, squeezing them twice, at an angle.

"Salaam?"

"Salaam."

Abudo already ought to know what his friend is looking for. The huts of Saua–Saua are dispersed but, for some strange reason, news of death or disgrace spreads rapidly, as if it is carried on the unquiet breeze that caresses the leaves of the mango trees. The two friends stare at each other for a moment and Mussa Racua understands imme-diately that the other already knows everything.

"Come in," invites Abudo.

Mussa Racua has to bend down a little to pass freely through the rough door painted in blue. That door is Abudo's pride, as are the two small window frames also painted in blue. A clear and shining blue, luxurious in contrast to the poverty of the rest of the hut, whose mataca mortar is already worn through in number of places.

The small room where Abudo takes his friend is clean and fresh, with the floor of compressed earth covered with a large grass mat. The only other furniture apart from the mat, the three–legged stool, the clay water jug and the catha for drinking water, is all neatly arranged in one corner.

The two friends sit on the grass mat, facing each other. An expectant silence hangs in the air, and even the very voices of the children who chatter in the yard sound distant and strange, like an echo.

"This is a bad year, brother," Abudo says finally, in the sweet Macua tongue.

Mussa Racua looks straight at him, gratefully. The friend wants to be saved at least from repeating the words he has been saying since morning, repeating in all the huts, repeating until they have almost lost all meaning.

"They tell me that you are walking in search of rice to give to the Administration."

"Since yesterday," responds Mussa Racua. "You are my final friend to whom I have come to ask for help. I know very well that I still owe you half a sack which you lent to me last year... Because of this I did not want to ask you again. But I have to pay. You know that I have to pay. I am two sacks short this year. Since yesterday I have been walking in search and found nothing. If you could organise two sacks for me, I..."

"This has been a cursed year. The rain almost didn't fall..." interrupts Abudo.

Mussa Racua does not hear what follows. He obstinately repeats the same words in short phrases, with sobs. Suddenly he realises that Abudo is gently rocking to and fro and his eyes are fixed on the mat.

'It's not worth continuing like this. He also cannot help me,' thinks Mussa Racua, seized by a sudden and inexpressible weariness.

He moves as if to stand up. Then, what his friend says leaves him paralysed as if he has been punched, unexpectedly, full in the face.

"I am also going to the plantation, brother! Like you and so many others this year."

"It can't be," screams Mussa Racua.

"Why not? I also could not supply the rice which they want. All that's left is that I have to go to the plantation," responds Abudo with a doleful calmness.

Mussa Racua stares at him open–mouthed. Finally overcoming his surprise, he moves a little closer to his friend and speaks to him, almost whispering.

"But you always manage to pull it off. The land they marked off for you is in a hollow. You were not left like me, always praying that the rain would fall. And why did you not go and ask your friends for help?"

"Yes I went! I went to see those who I thought could help. But this year, as you know, even they, most of them don't have rice enough to escape the plantation. Others only have sufficient to give to the Administration."

"Does your wife know?" asks Mussa Racua.

The other shrugs his shoulders like someone who considers it an irrelevant question.

"Yes, she knows. How could she not know?"

"Ah! Yes, it makes sense... She has to know... obviously! But haven't you thought what it will mean...Aren't you scared because you will not be here?"

Abudo doesn't answer. The anguish in the gestures and words of his friend begin little by little to break down the barrier of resignation that he had succeeded in building up inside himself, ever since he was certain that he would have to go to the plantation.

"How do you know that I'm not scared?" he asks finally. "But what can we do? Tell me! Can you show me anything that we can do?"

And these final words hover with bitter irony.

"I don't know anything! I only know that I won't cope with the plantation for a second time."

"But what can we do?" repeats Abudo, already with a trace of desperation in his voice. "Tell me, brother! It's the white man who orders it, how can you not go to the plantation if you do not have the rice that they want? If you run away you are caught with the others. And then they send you there every year. Almost everyone they catch ends up dying there. You well know that..."

"But you already know, brother, what life do we have left?" interrupts Mussa Racua. "Those people from the Administration come and mark a piece of land. Give us seeds that we didn't ask for and say: you have to get three sacks from here, or six or seven sacks, whatever is in their heads. And if for whatever reason we get sick or the rain doesn't fall, or the seed is bad, and we cannot supply the rice which they want, then off we go to the plantations. And the bosses of the plantations are happy because they get given the men to work, for free. And the people of the Administration are happy because they receive from the bosses of the Plantations a fee for every head they hand over. And it is us who are ready to collapse with fear and from work every single year. And we can't even look after our machambas which don't provide enough to eat."

Abudo listens with his head hanging, an impotent anger growing inside him.

"Listen!" continues Mussa Racua, with feverish excitement, "I have never spoken of that suffering. Everyone who has experienced the plantation never wants to speak of it again. The food is like shit! And even so it is barely enough for a man to cope with the work. And that sisal which never ends. That sisal has blood, brother, it's saturated with blood! The work always hurts. Pain and getting whipped. And after so much time, come from there with nothing... With nothing, brother! And here our few things without a man to protect them."

"But it has to be, brother, the white man orders it. What can we do? It's the white man who orders."

Abudo repeats the words like someone reciting a litany. Mussa Racua's eyes suddenly lose the agitation which has been animating them during the conversation with his friend. He would like to make him understand the complete horror of the plantation, but feels how poor his words of a simple man are.

'It's not worth the trouble,' he thinks with irritated hopelessness. 'It's not worth it.'

He thinks also that, if his friend has to leave, why should he feel more afraid? The plantation is the terror of all the blacks, even those who have never been there. Abudo has been a good friend. Many times he has saved him from the plantation by providing him with the rice left over after he had handed over the required amount to the Administration. Because of this he does not like to see him suffering beyond his strength. Because of the suffering of daily life, the constant certainty of not being anyone, the deep fear of the whites, all of this, he still believes it is possible to survive. But the plantation...

Mussa Racua gets up slowly from the grass mat. Only now does he notice that night has fallen completely and out there the nocturnal animals have begun their nostalgic concert. From the yard Abudo's wife brings a small paraffin lamp which she places on the three–legged stool. She greets Mussa Racua in a voice laden with sadness. It is as if she has been resigned-ly accumulating all the sadness of the world for centuries. This explains her vague greeting. It is as if she no longer exists in that house, as if she has already been swept away by the disgrace which hangs over her family.

"Okay, I'm leaving now," Mussa Racua suddenly bids in farewell, "good–bye!"

"Go with peace," Abudo wishes him.

The studied resignation of his friend violently irritates Mussa Racua who, without another word, goes through the blue door and dives into the night. He still has to cross a great distance to get to his hut, and he walks quickly, indifferent to the fresh nocturnal breeze and the familiar melody of the wild animals. His head is boiling with ideas and projects which come flooding in, without ever taking shape. He finally arrives at his hut. She has barely sat down to be with him and, on seeing him throw the empty sacks on the ground, understands that her husband will now have to leave for the plantations.

"Nothing! I achieved nothing!" Mussa Racua says simply.

He is standing, next to the door, and regards his Maiassa. His Maiassa, whom even the advanced state of her pregnancy cannot deform. She is, in reality, a beautiful woman, black as ebony, skin of silk, and languid and gentle, large eyes.

'I'm going to lose her,' thinks Mussa Racua. 'There is no young and beautiful woman who could bear to wait for a man who goes off to the plantation.'

And a deep and intolerable pain forces him to say brusquely:

"I'm tired. Bring me food."

He has no hunger at all. He has not eaten all day but he is not hungry. Nevertheless, he cannot bear the presence of his wife, waiting there for him to say something to her. He has nothing to say. He is going to the plantation, that's all. He is even on the verge of believing that he will shortly cease to be Mussa Racua, to become a species of working animal, from the break of day until sunset on the plantation of some white man. And that when he returns with his body scarred with new wounds, he will not find her. Could it be that if he told her this she would understand everything suddenly? Mussa Racua is not sure, even though Maiassa is a woman who understands many things. And because he is not sure and still does not know how to make her understand the depth of his despair, he rudely orders her to bring food.

After swallowing, with difficulty, the banana nimine which Maiassa has brought, Mussa Racua lies down on his quitanda bed. He can hear his wife out there washing the pots and the old aluminium pan out of which he is used to eating and he imagines the delicate and gentle gestures which are so dear to him. When she finally comes to lie down beside him, offering her body still fresh from the bath of the night, Mussa Racua embraces her tremblingly, through a strange mixture of desire and fury. Intuitively, Maiassa understands the despair he carries. And she manages to transform his pain with caresses of honey which calm him for a few short moments.

Only after his wife has gone to lie down on her bed does Mussa Racua, exhausted without sleep, think back and realise how much he has walked during the day. Every muscle of his body is in pain and his feet are throbbing, as heavy as lead. Nevertheless, his mind is alert, laboriously searching for a solution to his life. And, without wishing to, he remembers, one by one, the events of his previous experience on the sisal plantation.

He had been married for a short while to his first wife. Her name was Anifa and she was very young. The two worked tirelessly on their small machamba and on the rice machamba marked out by the Administration. Despite being so young, Anifa helped him like a real wife. They sowed the rice, transplanted it with care and harvested it. They did not eat nor waste a single grain. But even so, after the harvest, they only had five sacks. Much like this time, Mussa Racua visited the huts of all his friends and acquaintances, pleading with them to sell him the rice which he needed to supply to the Administration. But it had been a bad year, almost without rain, and no–one could help him.

He was still young without experience and, because of this, ingenuously, went to declare to the Administration that he could not supply the rice they demanded, due to the drought. He had worked so hard, he thought, that they would have to understand that it was through no fault of his own that he had brought so little rice. He was then taken into the presence of a white man. He was not the administrator, but someone authorised to decide on his behalf. The white man spoke slowly in Portuguese and the black Interpreter translated in shouts what the other was saying.

"You had to bring seven sacks, did you not?"

"That's right, yes," responded Mussa Racua. "I worked hard but could not make it because of the lack of rain."

The white man said something that the Interpreter translated into Macua in loud shouts.

"If you do not present the seven sacks which you have been ordered to, you will pay on the plantation. Do you hear? This conversation is ended. Do you hear? You can go now."

Yes, Mussa Racua had heard well. And he had also heard from others who had been there how hard life on the plantation was and how much misfortune was carried by the men who went there and left their homes. Others died there, without the comfort of their families. Others even returned blind. Just a little careless moment while cutting the sisal and there, a thorn threads its way through the eye of a man. And everyone returns ill and maimed, worn out from whippings and work without reward.

And now, stretched out on his bed, arms crossed behind his neck, feverish eyes fixed on the darkness, Mussa Racua still remembers those terrible days spent on the sisal plantation of Mister Fonseca. Only a few hours of sleep were possible. Despite the mosquitoes which infested the hostel where he slept with the other workers, despite the wounds from the whip which prevented him from being comfortable in any position, despite the extreme tiredness... But the hours of rest were always so short.

Mussa Racua cannot bear such memories without waves of real physical pain running through his body.

But, in spite of the effort that he makes to ward them off, they return again, insidious and bitter, hammering at his exhausted mind. And he still remembers his return...On the way he came to know that his wife had gone with another man to Matibane. She could not bear the long absence without news and without money. He also remembers how he found his empty house, the small machamba covered with grass, his few goats disappeared...

Brusquely, Mussa Racua sits up in his bed. Despite the cool night, beads of sweat cover his tense face and he trembles with pure indignation.

'No, no I cannot cope with such suffering all over again,' he thinks. 'There are others that can cope, but I can't. It's better to die. Not wake up ever again. Not be an animal ever again. Not return home again and see that my wife has gone with another man.'

And suddenly, the solution that he has been seeking for so long seems so simple, so natural, so obvious, that he is surprised he has not thought of it much earlier.

In the moonlit darkness of his small room he senses his wife sleeping an agitated but deep sleep. A violent desire to squeeze her in his arms forever drives him towards her, but he draws back half way across the room. Then, with feline movements, quick and silent, he goes out without a backward glance.

Maiassa only awakes with the first light of morning and, in an instant, gets out of bed. She vaguely remembers that she has to confront a great misfortune, but what?! The deep sleep of the pregnant woman still prevents her from thinking clearly. Only when she looks at the bed of her husband and does not see him, is it that she understands what has been worrying her.

'I'm a bad wife,' she thinks. 'My husband goes from here in a few days for the plantation and I'm still sleeping so much.'

She runs to wash in the chaorro in the yard. But when she returns to the room, she feels there is something not right. She does not hear the usual sounds of movement of her husband. Despite the happy choir of a flock of birds that sings in the nests hanging in the trees, the silence in the hut makes her heart heavy. Where could her husband be? Why has she not heard him this morning. She looks for him all around the hut, the yard, the chaorro, the small goat pen...

"Puapo nhum! Puapo nhum!" she calls, already concerned and anxious.

Only the twittering of the birds answers her. Seized with anxiety, she searches for her husband along the paths nearby the hut.

"Puapo nhum! Puapo nhum! Puapo nhum!"

Her belly weighs her down, but she begins to run as if she wants to arrive in time to prevent a disaster. Still running, she decides to go along the main road. But, little by little, the foreboding which has been growing in her chest is becoming a certainty. Now she neither runs, nor screams. She does not really know what has happened, but she feels that something beyond hope has taken place, that her husband has gone, that she will never have him again. And it is almost without surprise that, on doubling back on her path, she faces the body of Mussa Racua hanging from a mango tree, swaying gently in the sweet morning breeze. Fallen over on the ground, a full sack of rice.

Hours later, a wizened peasant dressed in tatters is presented almost forcibly in the office of the administrator. The man is constantly shaken by trembles which he is unable to suppress. The Interpreter, a bad–tempered man of mixed race, speaks on his behalf. He has already heard the whole story in Macua and now tells it in Portuguese.

"Early this morning," he says, " this man was walking along, when he saw a man hanged in a mango tree. He went closer and saw that it was one Mussa Racua. On the ground underneath him was a sack of rice fallen over and a woman who had fainted. It was the wife of said Mussa Racua. It was quite a job to get the woman to come round as she was in a deep swoon and..."

"Get a move on with this story," the administrator remarks impatiently.

These dramas of the blacks do not interest him, and even irritate him! Because of this he cannot bear the lengthy preamble of the

Interpreter. He, who enjoys translating in the finest detail, is disorientated by the haste of the administrator, and shuts up, incapable of continuing.

'Mother of god, I don't know where I was,' he thinks in terror.

"Are you continuing or not?" bellows the administrator.

The Interpreter makes an extreme effort to resume the story and proceeds in a disorganised fashion:

"Then the woman, when this man asked her why her husband hanged himself, she answered that it was because of rice."

"Because of rice?" exclaims the administrator, almost without wishing to.

Now this is beginning to get interesting. Rice is his business.

'There's that man interrupting again. Now I don't know where I was again,' thinks the Interpreter, discouraged.

And he hurries to end the story which, now resumed, he holds no interest in translating.

"Yes," he continues, speaking quickly. "He had to hand over eight sacks and only managed six. He went asking his friends but didn't manage anything. Because of this he obviously had to go to the plantation. And because he didn't want to go to the plantation, he hanged himself. And to hang himself he used a sack of rice. His wife stayed in her hut because she can't walk, but that is what she thinks, and that is what she told this guy."

He concludes the story pointing at the peasant who, standing there, looks on timidly.

"How many sacks did you say he could hand over?" asks the administrator after a moment, twirling a paperweight in his fat fingers.

"Six sacks, Mr Administrator," responds the Interpreter.

"Deal with fetching them as soon as possible. The seed was from the Administration and therefore the rice is rightfully ours. And do as is usual is such cases. Advise the sepoys."

"Very good, Mr Administrator. I will organise everything, Mr Administrator," cackles the Interpreter.

The wizened peasant dressed in tatters has not stopped trembling for all the time that he has been standing in front of the administrator. He understands virtually nothing of the conversation in Portuguese, but he waits constantly to be interrogated and is happy that this never happens. He was going to tell what he had seen because there is no other option. Nevertheless, he wants nothing to do with the people of the Administration and even less with the very administrator. It is therefore with a real sense of relief that he receives the order to leave and hurries to get out, in dread, dragging his thin and trembling legs.

Without seeing it, the administrator follows him with his eyes as far as the door. Then, returning to the Interpreter, but talking to himself, bursts out with an impatient anger:

"As soon as these dogs catch the scent of work they find some story. Either run away or kill themselves. Bloody blacks!"

Chaorro – outside wash stand

Macua – language spoken by tribe of the same name in northern Mozambique

Mataca – a mixture of sand and lime used as mortar

Machamba – plot of land used, usually, to grow food crops

Puapo nhum – my husband

Quitanda – bed made with wood and rope

Hassouna Mosbahi

✻

The Tortoise

Translated by Peter Clark

That was my first adventure. Before that adventure and afterwards, until I was a fourteen–year–old adolescent, they used to
beat me with a nail–studded stick that sometimes drew blood. There
was another stick, more slender, cut from olive or oleander. It twisted
like a leather belt and marked my back and thighs with red or violet
weals. With each stroke it hissed with pleasure or revenge – "Ayyah".
When I look back today I wonder how I managed to survive.

They used to beat me all the time. At funerals and on feast–days.
When it was cold, and during the afternoon siesta. Only when they
were tired or bored did they give up. There I would be, mouth agape,
bloody, unable to shout or to cry because of the acute pain. Everyone
took part – Father, Mother, my sister Bayyah, uncles, aunts. Even distant relations used to have a go. They said they had to make my worthy
of the family name and fit to be my grandfather's grandson. He had
been a noble knight, well regarded by plain and mountain, a man to
whom the tribes of west and east bowed in reverence.

When the blows were raining down on me I secretly appealed to
him. Perhaps he would deliver me from this awful pain. In writhing
agony I imagined him arriving suddenly on horseback, brandishing a
sword in their faces, shouting:

"Leave the boy alone, you swine."

They would turn tail, crushed. I would then stand at his side, tri-
umphantly watching their retreat.

But he remained silent, like the distant mountains that surrounded
our village. The earth remained the earth and the sky the sky, the same
as ever. With the passing of time and the increase of pain I grew to hate
him as I hated them. Indeed more than once I felt he was behind them,
blessing their deeds and spurring them in their abuse of me. When I
passed the cemetery I decided to go and piss on his grave. As I did just
that my whole body burnt and my head boiled like a cauldron. It was
as if the soil was grumbling and the heavens were mumbling in fury,

like some wild beast touched by evil. I then ran off, trailing clouds of rust–coloured dust. Thenceforth he occupied an obscure place in my heart and I grew to fear him as one fears ghosts or the worthy saints of Allah.

They all beat me. Father did it almost every morning. Sometimes he would bind my arms and legs and throw me into the barn all day or all night without food or drink. Or when I was some distance from him he would throw his stick at me as if I was some frisky or obstinate beast of burden. He would constantly say I was worthless or was the son of a dog, and his moustache would quiver like a thorn bush. I sometimes thought as I wandered among the olive fields in the autumn that I was perhaps not his son. Had I been found in some ditch or by the road-side? I had in mind a story told by al–Khatimi, Mother's brother. The central character was a child, abandoned by his mother near some village, who then fled to the mountains and lived a tough life, full of hardship and tears.

When I thought of that legend my sense of individuality grew. The world extended before me, dry and sad, filling my mind with fantasies and whisperings. I would sit under an olive tree, my head leaning against the trunk. I would sob and sob, no longer able to see what was in front of me.

Mother used to beat me before I went to bed and at mealtimes. Sometimes she would chase me, stick in hand, through olive fields, valleys and on the plain surrounding our village. When she got tired she would throw herself on the ground, sweating, with dry lips and shouting to anybody around:

"Grab him, the son of a dog. He's brought distress to his parents."

And Bayyah was my sister. She and I slept in the same bunk. I would go with her to the spring, to the olive fields, to the harvest. We gathered straw for the pack animals together. She showed me no pity and used to devise ways of beating me more than the others. Once she put my head between her thighs and smacked my bum until it felt as if it was on fire. And once she pummelled me like a lump of dough. She then sat on top of me and pushed down and down until the whole of my body was one big scarlet bruise. She used to pinch my ears so I had a fever at night. When she pinched my cheeks it was like a scorpion's sting in the heat of August. I hated her most when she tried to be like Mother, even more so when she stiffened and pursed her lips and stuck her nose in the air like some stern old lady. If only she were smaller than me, I would have exacted my revenge and thrown her onto the fire. I thought of killing her when she was sleeping in the bunk one hot afternoon, the flies buzzing around her, drawn by the smell of milk coming from her mouth. But some movement outside made me change my mind, I went off in anger to the olive fields.

On one occasion I did feel affection for her. She sang me a song she had memorised after some outsiders came to the village, erected some red flags and told us, "Rejoice. We are now independent." They all stood in a row and sang the song, with fists raised high. They then set off for the west, still singing, and stamping the ground in their black shoes, disappearing into the woods, their voices apparently suspended in space.

Bayyah used to sing this song as she followed the cow to pasture on spring mornings, full of light and sweet smells. All day she would sing, "Protectors, protectors, the glory of our age." And she would stamp the ground with her bare feet. Sometimes I would see her wander far away. She would blush and stare at the scrubland in the west. On that day I felt affection towards her and would like to have kissed her and hugged her. I wanted her to call me, put me on her lap and promise never to hit me again. But that evening as we came near our house she threw herself on me suddenly, and seized me by the neck as you seize a chicken when you are about to kill it. She then squeezed my neck so tightly that my tongue fell out as far as it could go and I felt as if my eyes were popping out. Mother then savagely called out:

"Go on, hit the dog until he gets things right."

Today when I call on her, she shows me the latest carpet she has woven. Her seven children crowd round me and she tells them:

"Look, this is your uncle. I've told you all about him. Look at him and be like him."

She then turns to me and says:

"If I thought you'd turn out like this I wouldn't have hit you so much."

I looked back and she was almost in tears.

"Forgive me, brother," she said. "I did love you, but I wanted you to be a man, a lord of men, as you've now become."

I stayed a day or two and then moved on. She stood still in her faded red dress, bidding farewell, her eyes full of tears of anguish.

They all beat me. None of them showed me the slightest sympathy, or gave me a kind word, even accidentally. They took pleasure in abusing me and abasing me, as if I were the cause of their hunger and thirst, the drought and their oppression, of the diseases of the olive trees and the beasts, the death of the wild figs before they had matured, and the other calamities that afflicted them over the years.

All, that is, except my aunt Fatima, who showed kindness and decency. She had a tattoo on her forehead and would kiss me when we met in the dry river bed, in the olive fields or at the spring. When I went to call on her she would give me some sweets and some *hulqum* and lots of other things. She would put my head on her knee and trace her fingers in my hair, looking for lice. When she found one she would kill it gleefully. She cursed Mother for her treatment of me, and Father for thinking only of his beasts and his animals. I hugged her and wanted to stay with her for ever. I once went to see her. She was grinding corn. She sat me beside her and sang to me:

Oh, my gazelle, I have brought you up.
How beautiful you are with your jet–black eyes.
This alone shows Allah's power
And has led me to you.

I felt that I was that black–eyed gazelle, wandering at liberty, browsing in valley and plain, without restraint and allowing nobody to come near. She would then sing other songs that transported me to distant lands, and filled my heart with loneliness and sadness. I would imagine I was a blade of grass in a raging storm. I then came to myself. Aunt Fatima was there, sobbing. I too was in tears, my head on her knee. When I went home that evening I felt that I and my aunt were outsiders in that cruel village.

Nowadays when I call on her I find her in a corner, shrunk and sightless. I approach her in silence. She feels me and smells me, and then repeats my name and throws herself at me, weeping and saying:

"Where are you, my fair gazelle? I have been told that you have crossed the seas and have gone to Frankish lands. What are you doing there? I always knew you were a bright lad. You do not forget us, my boy, you are a piece of my own flesh and blood."

That was my first adventure! Before that adventure and afterwards, until I was fourteen they would beat me and call me foul bastard, ass, Ibrahim's donkey – this Ibrahim was a neighbour who had a wretched obstinate donkey with a back that bled all the time. They called me mule's hoof, bitch's whelp, dung beetle and... many other things I have now forgotten. They would fall like stones on my mind, scald my body like knives and fill my soul with pitch. Sometimes I would take Mother's small round mirror and hide in the barn for an hour or so, gazing at the reflection of my face, with all these epithets mingling in my mind so it all became an ugly obscure mass. I then wept bitter tears, wishing I might never leave the barn. Once I saw my face in a muddy pool and almost cried out in fright. It was broad and dry like barren land or like the stones of cruel mountains. There were lines of snot and tears and furrows of pain and confusion. And one afternoon when I stretched out under an olive tree I saw Ibrahim's donkey surrendering itself as usual to the heat and flies. I went to look at it sympathetically and then I found myself – I don't know how – at its side, talking caressingly to it. But it paid no attention to me and stayed still, gloomy-eyed, loath to contemplate its own ugliness or the ugliness of the world around.

They used to beat me and say:

"May Allah gouge your eyes out. May He make your children childless. May He slam every door in your face and blacken your reputation and scatter every path you take with thorns. May you die in some remote mountain pass."

When they got tired of this or ran out of other misfortunes to wish for me, they would raise their hands and call on the Prophets and the Allah's worthy saints to answer their prayers. There would be no rhyme or reason for these curses. They would say:

"Why are you quiet all the time? Don't you have a tongue?"

When I spoke they would say:

"Why does your tongue go round and round like a fan?"

When I was up early,

"Why are you first up like a cock?"

And if I stayed up late with them,

"Do you want to learn bad habits, you bastard?"

If I smiled,

"Why do you laugh all the time as if we had no clothes on?"

And when I frowned,

"Why are you always glum and gloomy? Do you want to court misfortune for us?"

And so it went on. That is how things were with me. One morning I was recalling those days in the English Gardens in Munich. I began to laugh aloud and stamp my feet. Two old ladies were sunbathing in the warm April sunshine. A girl walked by exercising her dog. She was like a tailor's model in a shop window. Then there was a punk who was like an old hoopoe bird, laughing and spitting all the time. I laughed even more, and people scattered in alarm. The punk sat there some distance away and stretched out his legs like a dog at ease, breathlessly waiting for things to happen.

That was my first adventure.

Before then I used to wander in the fields and woods. I could capture jerboas in their lairs and surprise rabbits as they slept with open eyes and trap birds in their nests. I would spend ages doing these things. I would listen to noises, know when the olives turned black, when the almonds had bloomed, when the wheat yellowed with the ears nodding, when the wild figs ripened and turned red. I got depressed by the distant mountains that towered over our village in all directions, preventing me from seeing what was beyond. When people travelled east or west or north or south my heart went with them. When people talked about strange worlds filled with light and sound, with sweets and cakes I felt restrained and yearned to fly beyond the mountains. I memorised the names of the cities and villages they talked about. I repeated them to myself, intoxicated and breathless. I cursed those mountains. They were alongside the people who beat me and humiliated me all the time.

From the beginning I seemed strange and odd to my family. I hated watering the fields, getting hay for the donkeys or Indian figs for the camels. Whenever I did these chores I always feared the stick and the abuse. When I undertook any of these tasks I would make some mistake so they would think I was just daft, some dumb clown unfit neither for the world nor for religion, that I was some misfortune from which they suffered.

My happiest time was when I was stretched out beneath the olive tree gazing at the beauty of the heavens. Or when I disappeared into the barn, taking some charcoal to draw on huge copper pots shapes and lines like those I had seen on the writing–boards of the boys as they returned from the house of the schoolmaster.

At home they used to say that my uncle Mohammed had studied at the Zaituna Mosque in Tunis. They held him in awe and often sought his advice in matters of Allah and of man. He would walk with them, tall and broad, his tummy stuck forward and his fez tilted back and a cigarette always between his lips. But Father also said crossly that uncle Mohammed had all but impoverished the family and broken it up. They had sold six cows so he could become a respectable man of letters, bringing honour to the family. But he failed in his studies because of some snub–nosed woman from a western tribe whom he fell for. For her sake he came back to the village with huge trunks full of books and papers. I would look at these trunks, trembling with a desire to know what they contained.

One day, thanks to the carelessness of the snub–nosed wife, I opened one of them and took out the first book I touched. I hid it under my gallabiya and went off behind the cow. Father shouted at me, telling me to make sure the cow did not trample the crops. But as soon as I could I stretched out on my tummy under the warm spring sun. With shaking hands I opened the book and gazed with wonder at its lines and images. I soon forgot the world and what was in it. My mind wandered among lands that were violet and sky–blue, or the colour of red anemones. I was oblivious of everything until I felt a stick on my body and heard Father shouting and swearing at me. But for an elder of the village passing by he would have killed me that day. That night before I went to sleep he said to me:

"Listen, my boy, do you want to ruin the family like your uncle Mohammed did? If I come across you again with those books and papers in your hand I will roast you alive."

But I soon forgot his threats and went back to gazing at those trunks, my eyes glistening with desire, eager to know their contents.

One day I was looking after the cow as usual, and some lads came along carrying their writing–boards. I looked after them as they squawked like happy chicks and then I found myself – I don't know how – following them. Suddenly I noticed a cousin, slightly older than me. He shouted at me like one of the grown–ups:

"Go back to your cow, boy!"

When he went on threatening me, I picked up a stone.

"Listen to me," I shouted. "Leave me alone or I'll smash your head in."

Perhaps he thought I was serious, for he then ignored me. I went with them all to the schoolmaster's house, entered and squatted down like the rest of them. Soon their heads rocked to and fro and they mouthed those wonderful words. Then Father came in like a raging bull, with his stick, crazy and menacing. He said nothing to the school-master, totally ignoring him.

"Here, you dog," he shouted.

My cousin stood up, finding the chance of exacting revenge on an enemy, and pointed at me.

"There he is, uncle, in the corner," he said. "I told him to go back but he threatened me with a big stick."

I recoiled with terror and looked appealingly to the schoolmaster. My lips trembled and I was on the verge of tears. I saw a glint of sympathy in the schoolmaster's eyes, like a bird in the distance. Before Father reached me the schoolmaster seized his hand and led him gently to the door.

"Shame on you, Ibn 'Ali. Are you forbidding your son from learning the word of Allah?"

"The boy will being you pain and distress," Father shouted. "He has no idea what is behind him or what is in front of him. He's a disaster I've had to suffer from."

The schoolmaster put his hand on my shoulder.

"Leave him in my care," he replied. "Who knows? He may surprise us all."

For the first time I saw Father crushed. The stick was lowered. His eyes wandered awhile and he left, head somewhat bowed.

A few months later my cousin was having trouble reading one of the suras of the Qur'an. The schoolmaster's stick hovered over his head. My cousin froze like a mouse surprised by a cat, his lips quivering in search of the forgotten verse. When I felt he was lost I repeated the verse. I blushed in spite of a sense of elation I felt for the first time in my life. The other boys turned in my direction like calves that had been brought their feed. The schoolmaster lowered his stick and looked at me. There was astonishment in his features.

"Go on," he said.

And I went on, rocking forward and back. I continued and did not stop until I had finished the sura. He asked me to recite another sura. I did so without concern or hesitation. When I finished he gave praise to Allah and dismissed the other pupils. He took me by the hand and we walked in silence to our house. As we approached I could see Father stitching his smock, his stick at his side and a pot of tea before him. When he saw us he shouted:

"Now you know the son of a dog. I told you he was useless, fit only for a beating, didn't I?"

I tried to hide and clung to the schoolmaster's cloak. I waited for Father to jump up with his stick. But he remained engrossed in his stitching, muttering something I could not make out. We stood in front of him.

"Did I not tell you that your son would surprise us?" the instructor said proudly.

Father stopped stitching, looked up but said nothing.

"Listen, Ibn 'Ali," the instructor continued. "For twenty years I have been teaching the Qur'an around the place, but never have I come across a pupil like your son. Just imagine, he has learnt every sura just by listening."

He then repeated Surat al–Waqi'a to him. To prove his words he asked me to repeat it. I sat down, did so, and we wandered from sura to sura, my face pink, my head rocking.

But this incident changed nothing. They went on beating and abusing me until I was fourteen years old.

That was my first adventure.

That incident took place in the autumn when the village enjoyed itself. There was a togetherness among the people, who had happy, laughing, radiant faces. The rains at the end of August had banished that ugly barrenness that followed the harvest. Wild figs covered the ground with their lovely russet coat. Every night the plains and the hills echoed to the rhythm of drum and pipe, the chanting of women, the songs of the men and the firing of guns. At sunset the alleys were full of the bustle of excited young people as they went from wedding to wedding, looking for eyes that would burn their hearts in daytime.

One autumn day I was laying beneath the olive tree, dreaming as usual and contemplating the beauty of the world. Suddenly Ugly Salih was standing before me and asking me what I was doing.

The grown–ups were always telling us not to pass by blood or ashes without saying, "In the name of Allah". We were to shun the valley, fire, camels and not go near Ugly Salih. He was evil, disobedient, filthy and had a huge mouth.

I sat up ready to defend myself or to flee. I don't know why they called him "Ugly". Mother used to say that his family ate grass and wild figs, and that his father lost everything through gambling and quarrelling, and that his mother was a prostitute. Amazing stories were told about him. They said they found him once in the village of Makthar, and once in the village of Hajib al–'Ayun. Once he boarded a bus and went to Kairouan. I also heard them say he had stolen a chicken from Al–Askari and a turkey from Al–Muldi, and that he had split open Al–Gharbi's head with a stone. All this went through my mind while his lips shook continuously. But not a sound did he utter.

Again he surprised me.

"Listen," he said. "Do you want to come with me to al–'Ala?" It's market day tomorrow. If you like we can go at dawn and get back in the afternoon. Nobody will take any notice of us."

He described the market, and the donkeys, the sellers of hides and eggs, the vegetables, the crowded buses. "You're on your way to cities far away where you have cars – red, green and yellow, making a noise like women celebrating. We can eat honey–cakes and buy sweets and that white bread our families sometimes get."

He went on talking and talking. My mouth opened wide with

amazement until a fly found its way in and I was throwing up for an hour, feeling that my whole stomach was turning into one great black fly that carried the filth of the world.

Ugly Salih remained at my side, whispering. He seemed to be kind and good. He then took me again by surprise.

"Let's go and find a tortoise," he said.

"A tortoise?"

"Yes, a tortoise. They fetch a high price at the market, you know."

He put his hand into one of his huge pockets and brought out a handful of change.

"I've still got this left from the money I got from selling a tortoise last Thursday at al–'Ala."

I was dazzled and imagined that for the price of a tortoise I could buy the whole world. I saw myself coming home from al–'Ala with white clothes and black shoes like those men who came to the village and unfurled flags and then set off west, singing that beautiful anthem. The bad stories I'd heard about Ugly Salih vanished from my mind and I followed him without hesitation.

We wandered through valleys and scrubland. We climbed up and down, and went so far that we could see nothing of the village. We looked down on other villages that seemed sad and empty. I was afraid and wanted to go back. He reassured me, his eyes fixed firmly on the ground. We went so far that my legs ached and my throat was dry. The sun was sinking rapidly towards the western mountains, and twilight was cloaking the lower plain and the deeper valleys. Suddenly from behind a cypress tree his voice came to me:

"I've found them. I've found them."

I hurried up to him. His legs were wide apart and his mouth was huge. A blaze of triumph shone through his narrow eyes. There in the middle of nowhere was a huge tortoise.

"It's enormous," he said without moving. "We could buy the whole market with what we can get for this."

We hurried back. Near the village he whispered to me:

"Listen. Spend tonight in the barn. At dawn when the dogs begin to bark, get up and make haste."

After dinner I yawned and looked at Mother.

"You want to go to bed, son?" she said sweetly. "Go up to your bunk with your sister."

I did not move.

"Didn't you hear what I said?" she said crossly.

I hesitated a moment and tossed a hand grenade into their midst:

"I want to sleep in the barn."

"In the barn!" the three of them all shouted. They glared at me as if I had committed some heinous sin.

"Why in the barn, you wretch?" Father said.

My heart beat like a drum at the entry of the bride, and I said quickly: "I want to protect the cattle against robbers."

"You!" Father bawled. "Since when have you been old enough to protect us against robbers? Just get up to your bunk, you turd, and stop all this nonsense."

Bayyah looked at me.

"It's not cattle you're concerned about in the barn," she said. "Wait a moment."

She went out and returned.

"There's nothing in the barn. But there's something on his mind, I'm certain."

The bitch! Always in my way. I've cursed her many a time. I then quickly got into the bunk so they would not find out my secret.

"There's something on his mind," repeated Bayyah, "and I'm going to find out."

For a long time I tossed and turned, fantasising, my mind full of those delightful stories Ugly Salih had told me. Then I dozed off, I don't know how. When I woke up the dog was barking in great excitement. I so wanted to set eyes on that world of wonders, if only for an hour, and had been planning how to slip out without anybody noticing. I slid to the floor and Bayyah grabbed me from behind.

"Where are you off to, you bastard?"

"I want a pee."

"Do you really want a pee, or is it your secret in the barn?"

Before I could answer, human voices were mingled with the barking of dogs. The din got louder and louder and woke the whole village. When the barking died down I heard sobbing that was like a hungry animal. Then Father's voice thundered,

"You dog! What are you doing here?"

"I agreed with him to go to al–'Ala," whimpered Ugly Salih.

Bayyah pushed me towards the door. In the pale dawn light I saw the two of them. Father had a terrified, frail, misshapen, downtrodden Ugly by the scruff of the neck. When Father shook him the tortoise fell.

"What's this?" shouted Father.

"A tortoise."

"A tortoise?"

"We were going to sell it at al–'Ala market."

"Sell it at al–'Ala market?"

"Yes."

Father got angrier and beat him and then threw him to one side as if he were a datestone, and turned to me.

"You want to sell a tortoise? What are people going to say about us when they see you at the market of al–'Ala selling a tortoise?"

Then I was attacked on both sides, Father in front and Bayyah from behind. From a distance Mother egged them on.

"Beat him until the wretch knows right from wrong."

For two days after that I was bound hand and foot. Every hour one of them came to give me my quota of kicks and beatings.

That was my first adventure.

At the age of fourteen I obtained a primary school certificate, and police in a jeep came and told Father I had got first prize. They took me with them to Kairouan.

When I returned I found collections of stories of Kamil al–Kailani and Hans Christian Andersen. Mother wept with delight.

Bayyah wept for joy. Father looked at her distantly and then gave me a look and I realised that I had grown up and that none of them would ever beat me again.

One cold February day father collapsed in a field as he was looking after the cattle. They brought him home and when people gathered round he said:

"I want my son."

I was in Kairouan. The telegram arrived in the morning. I was home by noon. He looked at me for a long while.

"Read me something from the book of Allah, my son," he said.

I read five suras to him: al–Rahman, Yasin, Al–Baqara, Yusuf and al–Nisa.

When I finished he took my hand and said:

"I can now die in peace."

His eyes then closed for the last time.

hulqum – sweet similar to Turkish delight

⁂

The Wanderer

Translated and abridged by Peter Clark

He betrayed his Bedouin forbears in everything except their love of nomadic wandering. When he was a child his mother used to point to the broad plains and the bare hills. "I gave birth to you over there," she would say.

He gazed at her long pale face, her slender body and her light green wraparound: she was like an olive tree in a season of drought.

"Whereabouts exactly?" he asked.

She always pointed at the plains and the hills and repeated her words as if she had not heard the question.

"I gave birth to you over there."

He too looked at the distant horizon, where the hills seemed to be like waves or clouds of thick grey dust. He clung to her dress.

"But where exactly?" he pleaded. "Tell me, whereabouts exactly."

"I can't remember exactly," she said, as if talking to herself. "You know, we had to move camp from time to time, depending on the time of the year. But you were born at the beginning of autumn. I think I gave birth to you near the great Camel olive tree, but no... no, I think it was in the week of the afreets. At the foot of the Red Mountain. Or maybe... Oh, I've forgotten. Memory is as faithless as a man, my boy."

He spent days wandering over the plain and in the hills looking for the place where he had first seen light. He despaired of ever finding it, went back to his mother and plucked at her dress.

"Where was it exactly?" he insisted. "Exactly where?"

On one particular autumn day when the flies were buzzing and the air was heavy with the yellow dust that had been brought in by the scorching winds from the south, his mother got fed up with his questions, shook a stick in his face and shouted at him.

"Just stop asking questions, wretched child," she said. "Or your head will meet this stick. I've told you a thousand times, I can't remember. I simply can't remember. Haven't you heard what I said?"

He curled up in a corner, trembling. She stood there, her bosom heaving. Beads of sweat glistened on her long pale face. She tossed the stick aside.

"I can't remember the spot," she said, somewhat distracted. "But I do remember it was a difficult birth, and that when I was in labour Salim al–Ahmar was killed by a bomb left behind by the Germans during the war, and that a lot of donkeys and other animals died from some disease nobody knew anything about."

He was scared of the thick stick and shaken by the tales of disaster his mother had told so briskly. He did not dare ask any more questions. But they stayed in his mind as he sat reciting the Qur'an to his feeble one–eyed teacher. He used to spend half the day wandering over the plain. He climbed up the foothills of the mountains, and wandered aimlessly through the parched sandy wadis looking for some clue to the place of his birth. One day, exhausted, he stretched out in the shade of the Camel olive tree and turned things over in his mind. Thoughts galloped through his mind like horses at the races held to celebrate weddings. By sunset he had come to the conclusion that all things around him, great and small, were also totally unaware of their place of birth. They gave the question no importance whatsoever. All that concerned them was moving on. People were on the go all the time. In times of heat and in times of cold. On mountains and in deserts. At night and in the daytime. They ate as they moved on. They sang as they moved on. They quarreled as they moved on. Anything happened as they were on the move or were preparing to be on the move. His cousin Zainab gave birth when she was gathering corn in the middle of the afternoon. And Shaykh al–Hudhaili dropped dead as he was eating couscous and talking to guests. And Mabruk fell in love with Salima from the Masa'id tribe on his way back from some long journey to the north. And Hajj Salih, so it was said, walked to the holy city of Mecca and died there after having completed the rites of the pilgrimage. They were always on the move, like the wind. They were on the move as they sniffed the air for the smell of water or of fresh pastureland, like wolves sniffing out the scent of sheep. As his father used to say, "We're Bedouin. We only cease being on the move when we're thrown into the grave."

From then on he no longer thought about the place of his birth. But he wandered in his imagination, dreaming of the moment when he could set off beyond the mountains and return with wondrous tales of maids with shocks of fine hair who wandered barefoot through gardens of jasmine irrigated by rivers of milk and pure honey.

He then became fascinated by the tracks left by herds of goats in the hills, or the footprints of the shepherds in the wadis. Or the paths that led through the olive groves, tracks that spread out and joined up like a spider's web. But most of the tracks that stimulated his imagination were those that led far away, beyond the mountains. There another world began, a world his soul yearned for.

These tracks all had names, like human beings. The track that headed south was called the Long Road because it stretched out until it was lost in the far distance. From this track on cold winter days came beggars wrapped in light–coloured shabby burnouses. They looked like pathetic donkeys in a state of collapse. They wandered through our village and to the rhythm of tambourines chanted praise to God, with the aim of obtaining alms from the people.

At sunset people brought them bowls of couscous and meat. All night you could hear them, their voices rising and falling with the sighing of the wind and the beat of the tambourines.

The path that headed eastwards was called the Red Road, from the colour of the soil. From this track came men with tall gaunt frames, with faces as sharp as knives, sporting proud moustaches. They had tiny suspicious eyes, full of cunning. People would whisper to each other that they were thieves from the Mahafiz tribe who stole animals from the western tribes to sell in the markets of the east after dyeing them a different colour.

The path that headed northwards was called the Snakes' Road because of the number of poisonous snakes that could be found in the sulphurous crannies in hills crossed only by the bold and determined. Along this path came scowling tar merchants riding ugly mules. He loathed them and used to hide in a haystack as soon as he saw them coming. He once dreamt that they took him through the village tarred and naked, cracking their whips on his skull, with people around clapping and singing as if they were at a wedding.

But the most famous path was the Camel Road. First it led slowly and uncertainly through the wadis to the west of the village. It then suddenly rose, like a horse rearing its head in preparation for a fight. It climbed into the hills that divided their tribe from the Masa'id tribe. It then became lost in the black wilderness of the Empty Canyon. It derived its name from the fact that it was the camel caravan route to and from the west. In times of drought and hardship the caravans would fill the road with their cries and songs day and night. As they headed west he would climb up the lofty Camel olive tree. From its branches he would watch the caravan as it disappeared and became a dark blotch beneath a cloud of dust. That blotch remained in the middle of nowhere, apparently motionless, and then disappeared completely in that stretch of land called the Empty Canyon. It would leave the memory of its heavy groaning movements. People told strange and scary stories about the Camel Road. They said it was haunted by ghouls and spirits. Shaykh al–Ashhab, who was always on the move, used to tell various stories, full of detail, tales that could frighten old and young alike.

"Listen, my friends," one story started. "You know that from my youth I have travelled day and night, summer and winter. You know that I fear none but God the All–Knowing, the All–Capable. But I have unquestionably encountered fear more than once on the Camel Road. Yes, only on the Camel Road, and on no other road at all."

Shaykh al–Ashhab cleared his throat. His eyes scoured the horizon for a few minutes.

"One moonlit night, my friends," he resumed, "I was traversing the Empty Canyon. My mind was calm and I was moving slowly. Now and then I hummed some song. Then I sensed I heard the sound of a human in great distress. I stopped and listened carefully. There was no sound in this wilderness but the rustle of leaves and the rush of the wind. I murmured a prayer against Satan and continued my journey. Then a few paces on I heard a woman crying piteously for help.

"God, please do not kill me. Brother, do not make my little ones orphans."

"I took my knife out and had my stick in my hand. Cautiously I headed in the direction of the voice. Suddenly I heard the woman's cry for help again. But this time it came from another direction. I went towards it. The cry came again but I could not work out where it was coming from. I stopped in the middle of the track, my stick raised high. I stayed like that for some time, listening out for anything apart from the beating of my own heart. I moved again, and again the woman's voice was quite near me. It seemed to be between my feet.

"Dear God, please do not kill me. Brother, do not make my little ones orphans."

"It is not easy, my friends, to describe my feelings during those moments. Fear can, you know, blind a man and take his mind away. I recall only that I ran straight ahead, the woman's cries now between my feet, now behind me, now in front of me, to my left, to my right. She did not give up until a Masa'id dog started barking."

Shaykh al–Ashhab fell silent. He stared at the silent faces of the men around him.

"On one other occasion," he went on, "it was broad daylight, yes, in the middle of the day; I was making my way down the Wolves' Slope and suddenly came upon a woman of the most unparalleled beauty. Friends, she was as fair as a full moon. She was walking along, her face uncovered, her dark tresses cascading to her waist. She hastened to be right at my side.

"Are you of mankind, or are you a djinn?" I asked.

"I am of mankind, one of the best."

"Where are you from? Who are you? What are you doing here, all alone in this deserted place?"

"I am from the Masa'id, and have come out for a particular reason."

"How is it that your people let so fair a maid as yourself come uncovered and alone into such a wilderness?"

"This is a secret I will disclose to nobody," she laughed.

"Then she quizzed me about my background and my life. Charmed by her laughter and her sweet manner, her beautiful voice and her gracious way of moving, I replied. Then for some unknown reason I looked down at her feet. What I saw amazed and terrified me. This most gorgeous woman had the hooves of a mule. Yes, the hooves of a mule. I said to myself, 'Maybe heat and exhaustion have got to me, and sapped my wits'. I rubbed my eyes hard and stared at her again. I found myself facing a creature who had the head of an owl as well as the hooves of a mule. I don't know what I did after that. All I remember is that when I regained consciousness I was lying on the ground with men from the Masa'id tribe around me, sprinkling water on my face and invoking the name of God.

He betrayed his Bedouin forbears in everything except their love of nomadic wandering.

He grew up listening to wonderful stories. The most enchanting was the tale of his ancestress, Mahbuba. That story was told all the time, especially in the winter when it got really cold and folk gathered around the fire. Or on summer nights when they stayed up, stretched out on the threshing ground beneath a sky made bright by the most beautiful moon ever seen.

"It was in a year of severe drought," it was related, "when the Reaper had taken his generous harvest. The survivors of the tribe packed their few possessions onto camels, on donkeys and mules, left their homeland and set off to the distant east. They travelled day and night for months, fleeing dust, hunger and thirst. One night they rested at the foot of a mountain. At dawn they rose and resumed their trek. But one woman, Mahbuba, was accidentally left behind. Her husband had died on the road, leaving her with twin boys, Sa'ad and Sa'id. It was the middle of the morning when she woke up and found they were all alone in this vast emptiness. She was panic–stricken and ran around as one possessed, her two little ones babbling away on her back. She tired herself out, sat by the track and wept bitter tears. But God is merciful to his faithful people. He allows none to be forsaken. So, not long before the sun went down the poor woman saw before her a proud man with a face full of compassion. He asked her some questions.

"I've lost my way, good sir," she said, fighting back her tears. 'I've lost my family and my fellow travelling companions."

"She then told him her story in detail. He invited her to his house. He treated her respectfully, letting her forget that she was a stranger and a widow. She entered his service loyally and honourably.

When the twins grew up the good man summoned them.

"You are now two handsome young men,' he told them. 'From this day on you must show people what you are made of."

"He then gave each one of them a plot of fallow land on which there were only stones and thorns.

"If you put this land to good use,' he said, 'God will put you to good use."

"The twins toiled night and day, in heat and in cold, until that barren piece of land became green and fertile, and full of good things. When the wise old man saw this, he summoned them to him once more.

"God has prospered you in what I bade you undertake,' he said. 'You are entitled to take half what is due to you."

"He then married them to two wondrously fair young women from among his relations, arranging such a wedding party that people talked of it for many years afterwards."

At this point, the listeners fell silent, sat up in their seats, their skull–caps askew, and took a sip of their tea. One man sighed.

"God was merciful to our ancestress," he said, "as was the shaykh who looked after her and provided this fine wedding feast."

They then closed their eyes and sank into silence or into sleep. But our hero, in his fantasies, wandered far afield. He saw himself like Mahbuba, lost in the deserts where no man trod, where no bird flew. Nothing but stones, thorns, mirages. He was walking, walking, walking, crossing deserts, mountains and wadis, until he reached the land of ghouls. There he met ferocious robbers who would steal even the teeth of dogs as they barked. He met snakes that would swallow a man in an instant as if he were a fly. And crocodiles who could devour the

Sultan's army. And evil grey–haired witches who could turn men into monkeys or rats. After a fierce struggle he plunged his sword into one ghoul and returned on the back of a green horse that had wings of light, accompanies by a princess veiled by her long hair and carrying a scented apple that could restore youth and raise the dead.

He betrayed his Bedouin forbears in everything except their love of nomadic wandering.

On cold mornings he went to the Qur'anic teacher who chanted softly *"Glory to Him, who carried His servant by night from the Holy Mosque* to the Further Mosque**"*. He would repeat these strange words until he became totally oblivious to the cold, the thorny cactus plants and the evil one–eyed teacher whose stick hovered over their heads all day long. He saw himself standing in the desert with the most beautiful horse in the world – it had the face of a human, a mane of moist pearls alternating with luminous sapphire, ears of emerald and eyes like lustrous stars. It was grey–white, with three white feet and on its fourth an anklet studded with pearls. An unknown voice whispered to him "Mount and ride". And so he mounted and rode. The steed flew with him beyond the mountains surrounding his homeland. He looked down on people who were like ants. Then in one second they were in the seventh heaven. He looked below to see the earth and all that was on it as small as a drop of water.

Then one day he set off on his first journey. His mother stood on the doorstep, murmuring prayers to herself. His father leapt onto the back of their grey mule and issued instructions about the animals and about household matters. He jumped up behind and they set off. Behind them his mother poured out a bucket of water, saying not a word. At the edge of the village they found other men on mules waiting for them. They all set off slowly on the Camel Road. It was towards the end of an autumn day. Shadows covered the plain, the slopes and the mountains. The scent of fresh wild figs was in the air and the land had been stripped after the harvest. The sun set before they had traversed those bare wadis that divided them from the lands of the Masa'id. The darkness gradually thickened until the hills and mountains were transformed and they seemed suspended in space. At one point they were attacked by wild dogs but the men took no heed of them.

Mabruk Ould 'Amir told stories about his stingy grandfather that made them shake with laughter on the backs of their mules. Every now and then one of them would call out, "Tell us another, Mabruk. May you live long!"

They started to descend a rough slope. A cold wind, bearing the scents of pine, wormwood and juniper, brushed against them. The mules slowed down their ambling pace. The path straightened up. Shadowy trees intertwined above their heads.

As they went deeper into the forest it got colder and colder. As night drew on Mabruk's enthusiasm waned. Anecdotes became fewer and the gaps between them increased. They then stopped completely. His father and the other men were silent. All he could hear was the tramp of the hooves of the mules on the ground. Silence took such possession that he felt totally separated from his father and the other men. It was as if he was left floundering alone in the eternal darkness. Suddenly they heard a strange noise, and suddenly all was silent again. The forest then moved as if wild horses were charging through it. There were bizarre groans, and distressed bleats as of a camel about to be slaughtered. It seemed to the boy that the darkness was full of those spirits and ghouls and she–demons they had been talking about. He was about to cry out in terror, and then heard Mabruk:

"Dawn has broken, my friends."

It was while he was travelling with his father in the villages of the north that he became fascinated with atlases.

August. The horizons were lit up with the heat of mirages. He was puffing like a wild dog. His father was snoring loudly in a corner of the tent. His mother was grinding wheat and repeating those sad songs that recalled the motion of caravans as they made their slow heavy way towards the north. He knew that she would shortly burst into tears. Grief gathered in her heart like dust on a track. He slipped away with a huge atlas that he had won as a school prize for outstanding work. He stretched out in the shade of the Camel olive tree. Bliss! The branches chattered with those affecting songs that made him forget the grief–laden songs of his mother. As soon as he opened the book he forgot about everything else. He wandered through countries, crossed seas and oceans. Penetrated jungles. Here near the arm of his own country that stretched into the sea was the island of Sicily, shaped like the sheepskin that his mother would spread for visitors. Sardinia was shaped like an old tortoise. Beyond were the snow–covered Alps over which Hannibal's armies rumbled like a wild storm. To the left lay Gibraltar. Above lay the land of Andalus, drenched in the blood of defeated Arabs. Below that, red Marrakesh with its veiled Sultans and the roads to Timbuktu. He repeated to himself the name *Timbuktu, Timbuktu, Timbuktu,* as if he was repeating a favourite song. He traced with his fingers the desert roads that meandered and linked up in the places where troupes of blacks sang, their teeth as sparkling bright as stars on a dark night. Further down he could smell the African jungle, where crocodiles and lions were as much at liberty as the donkeys in his home village. At the heart of Africa was the Congo, blown up like the body of a ghoul. Then far away were the Magellan Straits where fierce storms blew all the year round. After wandering in those lands scattered on the edge of the world – Australia, the Philippines, Singapore, Malaysia, Ceylon – he turned back and looked at the Nile as it sauntered through the desert.

He was now not far from the land of revelation. *Glory to Him, who carried His servant by night from the Holy Mosque to the Further Mosque.* He pondered over the effects of the remarkable stories of the Qur'an. Here Moses cast his staff that turned into a snake. There was the pit into which Joseph was thrown. Here Abraham contemplated sacrificing his son, Isma'il. And here was the dry palm–tree to which Mary resorted at the time of her labour. There are the wells of Zamzam, the cave of Hira where Gabriel addressed the Prophet one dawn. He returned to Khadija in a feverish sweat, crying "Cover me up, cover me up."

Once more an old dream recurs, and he sees himself as a traveller, a staff in his hand, like Moses. He goes into the desert at night and the road is lit up for him as far as the eye can see. He is thirsty and his staff guides him to a well and he draws up water in a bucket. He needs food and strikes the ground and, lo and behold, before him is a table spread with all that is good and tasty. He wants some fruit. He strikes the ground again and at once a fruit–bearing tree springs up. He passes by a difficult mountain. He strikes the ground and a path opens up. He wishes to cross a river and dry land opens up before him.

He was in this dream world when the young lads of the village turned to him. "What have you been reading in that book?" they ask.

When he was fifteen years old he saw the sea for the first time. From that moment on he was so enchanted by the blue of the sea and the music of the crashing waves, that he developed a feeling of loss when he went back to the village. Over the course of time this sense of alienation intensified. He felt constrained by the desert winds, by the flies and the intense heat, the locusts, the crows that screeched on peaks, and by the snakes that hissed in the rocky hills when it was hot and by the lice that fed on the unwashed scalps of young people, by the snuff the Bedouin used to cram into their cheeks and up their noses, by the drought that destroyed man and beast and by the yellow dust that blinded people in the month of May.

This was indeed a break. He entered the capital by its southern gate one autumn afternoon when the sky was clear and the air was fresh. He dropped off his suitcase and wandered by himself among the book-shops near Bab al–Bahr and experienced a yearning for those books he had heard of but had not yet read: *Journey to the End of Night*, *A La Recherche du Temps Perdu*, *A Portrait of the Artist as a Young Man*.

"I must devour all these as soon as I can," he said to himself as he carried a bundle of books to the small room he shared with a huge stu-dent called Jum'a. He never tired of reading Che Guevara's memoirs or *The Little Red Book* of Mao Tse–tung. He dreamed of a new revo-lution that would bring workers and peasants to power. As for himself, he said to himself as he listened to Jum'a's fiery talk, "You are a Bedouin and have got to work hard to be a writer. Isn't this what you've wanted since you became besotted with atlases and ancient legends?" He closed his eyes and let his imagination wander. He could see his own books lining the windows of bookshops and people rushing to buy them. He saw himself sitting in Café Paris with city notables, smoking a pipe and replying calmly and eloquently to journalists' questions. Jum'a would bring him up sharp and shout: "You're betraying your class. You should be ashamed of yourself."

Then he met Yassin. He too liked to eat macaroni with spicy sauce in Maltese restaurants. He like the stories of old Mahmoud in the port bar, the girls of La Marsa and La Goulette in their summer swimming costumes. He enjoyed the films of Eisenstein, De Sica, Bergman, Pasolini, Jean–Luc Godard and Youssef Chahine. The poetry of Baudelaire, Rimbaud, Abu Nuwas, Lorca, Mayakovsky, Eluard and Adonis. The obsessions of Mersault on the beach of Algiers and Bloom in the brothels of Dublin. Like Yassin he loved Jewish songs and the music of al–Hadi al–Juwaini.

But it was his wanderlust that was stronger than anything else. He felt that the capital, the whole country, was too confined for his dreams. One restless day he and Yassin were drinking beer slowly at the Café des Negres.

"I'm going to travel," he announced.

"Where to?"

"I only want to get away to the West."

"What about the East?"

"That's like some old whore's cunt."

After that he crossed the seas and again there was a break in his life. For many years he wandered from country to country. In Paris he sought out what remained of the surrealists. He loved Chantal who dreamt of life amongst the Tuareg. In Madrid late one night he met a feeble old man who told him the details of Lorca's death. In Dublin he drank Guinness until he staggered about like a hero of Joyce. In Amsterdam he fell in love with a blonde girl who loved hashish, Berber songs and Arabic music. In New York he lived with the blacks and looked for traces of Henry Miller in Brooklyn. In Rome he shared foul wine and smelly cheese with revellers. In Copenhagen he heard that the security forces back home had killed hundreds in clashes with the trade unions. In Ronda he stayed quietly in the hotel Rainer Maria Rilke used to stay in. In Prague he was haunted by Kafkaesque nightmares. In Athens he dreamt that Socrates, wearing the clothes of an imam, chased him into the wilderness with a cudgel shouting: "Go back where you came from, go back, you rogue!" In Berlin he fathomed the pessimism of Schopenhauer: Life is like a pendulum, swinging from right to left, between pain and boredom.

* Holy Mosque – of Mecca   ** Further Mosque – of Jerusalem

This excerpt from *Tarshish Hallucination*, translated from the Arabic by Peter Clark, is reprinted with permission of *Banipal*, magazine of Modern Arab Literature in English translation from its double issue No. 10/11 Spring/Summer 2001 (Banipal, P O Box 22300, LONDON W13 8ZQ, UK)

Biographies

Mia Couto was born in 1955 in the northern port-city of Beira, Mozambique, but lives in Maputo, where he works as a journalist. He has been a director of the Mozambique Information Agency and is noted for his regular 'cronicando' newspaper columns in *Notícias*, which use literary forms to comment on current affairs. Several collections of his stories have been published, the first of which was published in Mozambique in 1986, and is now available in English as *Voices Made Night* in a translation by David Brookshaw. Other items in English have appeared in *Critical Quarterly*, *Third World Quarterly* (1990) and *New Era* (1991). *The Russian Princess* first appeared in an English version by Luís Rafael in *Staffrider* (Johannesburg, 1993), was collected by Bartlett in *Short Stories from Mozambique*, and then considerably revised for inclusion in *The Picador Book of African Stories* (London, 2000). It is also in Brookshaw's second collection of Mia Couto stories, *Every Man is a Race* (Heinemann African Writers Series, 1994).

Nuruddin Farah was born in 1945 in Biadoa in the Italian-administered south of Somaliland, which was united with the British north at independence in 1960. In the 1970s, he produced eight novels, starting with *From a Crooked Rib* in 1970, and in 1986, published another novel, *Maps* (Picador). His recent novel, *Secrets*, was published in 1998 and won that year's Neustadt International Prize for Literature. In 1999, the New York Review of Books described him as 'the most important African novelist to emerge in the last twenty-five years'. The first draft of his story, *The Affair*, appeared as *The Green of my I-Ps*, in *Bananas* (London, August 1980), but was revised for inclusion in *The Picador Book of African Stories*. Nuruddin Farah is at present based in Cape Town.

Helon Habila was born in Kaltungo, Gombe state, Nigeria, in 1967. He read Literature at the University of Jos, and then lectured in English and Literature at The Federal Polytechnic, Bauchi, from 1997 to 1999. He wrote for *Hints Magazine*, in Lagos, where he anchored two popular columns, *Campus Blues* and *Opinion*. Helon Habila's sto-ries have appeared in anthologies in Nigeria, the first being *Embrace of the Snake*, in the collection *Through Laughter and Tears*, edited by Chidi Nganga, in 1992. His first book was a biography, *Mai Kaltungo*, (1997). Helon Habila also writes poetry. His poem, *Another Age*, came first in the MUSON Festival Poetry Competition 2000. Two of his poems, *After the Obsession*, and *Birds in the Graveyard*, have been selected for publication in the upcoming anthology, *25 New Nigerian Poets* (Ishmael Reed, Berkeley, California). *Love Poems* appears in *Prison Stories* (Epik Books, Lagos, 2000), an anthology of his short sto-ries. He is now Arts Editor of *Vanguard Newspaper*, Lagos.

Lília Momplé was born in 1935 on the Island of Mozambique, which lies off the northern coast of the mainland. She went to sec-ondary school in the old Lourenco Marques and lived and worked in Lisbon, London and in Brazil, before returning to Maputo in 1981. She has since published a collection of short stories, *Ninguem Matou Suhura (No One Killed Suhura)*, in which the original of *Celina's Banquet*, translated by Richard Bartlett, was included.

Hassouna Mosbahi was born in Kairouan, Tunisia, in 1950. In 1968, he was awarded a Tunisian radio prize, and in 1986, he won the Prix National de la Nouvelle for his first volume of novellas published in Tunisia. Since 1985, Hassouna Mosbahi has lived in Munich, where he works as a writer, literary critic and freelance newspaper journalist. He has published a total of 11 books in Arabic and German: four vol-umes of short stories, three novels, a travelogue and some non–fiction. The German edition of his first novel, *Tarschisch Hallucination*, trans-lated by Regina Karachouli, (published as *Ruckkehr nach Tarschisch*, A1 Verlag, Germany, 2000) won the Munich Tucan Prize for best novel of 2000. His latest novel, *Adieu Rosalie*, was published in Germany this year (Dar al-Jamal, Cologne). *The Tortoise (Al-Sulhufat)* appeared in a collection of short stories of the same name (Dar Gilgamesh, Paris, 1996), translated by Peter Clark. The version for which Mosbahi is shortlisted was published in the Autumn 1999 issue of *Banipal* maga-zine.

Rules of the Caine Prize

The Prize is awarded annually to a short story by an African writer published in English, whether in Africa or elsewhere. (Indicative length, between 3 000 and 15 000 words).

"An African writer" is normally taken to mean someone who was born in Africa, or who is a national of an African country, or whose parents are African, and whose work has reflected African sensibilities.

There is a cash prize of $15,000 for the winning author and a travel award for each of the short-listed candidates (up to five in all).

For practical reasons, unpublished work and work in other languages is not eligible. Works translated into English from other languages are not excluded, provided they have been published in translation, and should such a work win, a proportion of the prize would be awarded to the translator.

The award is made in July each year, the deadline for submissions being 31 January. The short-list is selected from work published in the 5 years preceding the submissions deadline and not previously considered for a Caine Prize. Submissions should be made by publishers and will need to be accompanied by twelve original published copies of the work for consideration, sent to the address below. There is no application form.

Every effort is made to publicise the work of the short-listed authors through the broadcast as well as the printed media.

Winning and short-listed authors will be invited to participate in writers' workshops in Africa and elsewhere as resources permit.

The above rules were designed essentially to launch the Caine Prize and may be modified in the light of experience. Their objective is to establish the Caine Prize as a benchmark for excellence in African writing.

For further information, please contact Nick Elam at The Caine Prize for African Writing, 2 Drayson Mews, London W8 4LY. Telephone +44 (0) 20 7376 0440 Fax +44 (0) 20 7938 3728 e–mail: caineprize@jftaylor.com